CW00867681

DIRTY PANES

Confessions

of a

Window Cleaner

Richard Pane

Tellwell Talent
www.tellwell.ca

ISBN
978-0-2288-7999-2 (Hardcover)
978-0-2288-8000-4 (Paperback)
978-0-2288-7998-5 (eBook)

TABLE OF CONTENTS

INTRODUCTION

I've destroyed relationships: others' and mine. I was unfaithful to my own, and this of course eventually destroyed my relationships with my girlfriends at the time. Later, after I was married, I again destroyed my marriage with my infidelity. The seeds of my behaviour had been sown in 1985. I didn't realise it at the time, but that year turned me into a sex addict or something. Always on the prowl for my next sexual liaison. Wanting it to be hotter, dirtier, sleazier, louder, sneakier, and just plain naughtier than the previous. I was a walking penis, 24/7, always thinking about it, always wanting it. I just loved to fuck or having my cock sucked and jerked—whatever, really. I also really loved the hunt, the thrill of the chase, and the nervous anticipation before getting down and dirty. The raised heart rate, the blood rushing to my cheeks and my cock, and of course taking a woman completely and enjoying her giving in to me totally. That was the best feeling of all, and it's always what I was after. I really loved to drive my cock in a woman, and the first penetration was just the best sensation, as was the rest. I had developed quite a knack for picking up a bit of skirt if the mood took me, and it always took me, especially if I saw one I liked. If it didn't come to me, then I hunted it down. In my new career as a window cleaner, I was suddenly put in situations that never would have presented themselves to me. Lots of lonely ladies looking for some excitement, romance, and sex. Well, I gave them the sex, at least. The real sex, not the type they got with their husbands or boyfriends. I gave them something much naughtier and prohibited, and it's what they really desired. I gave them the sex they fantasised about and would remember fondly when I was no longer around.

As a young man in my early twenties, I spent two years working for a professional window cleaning company in some of the nicest suburbs in my city. What I ended up doing was a whole lot more than cleaning windows. I entered the lioness's den, and she was purring.

I have done many things in my life, sexual misadventures being a continuous theme. In 1985 I started to catalogue many of these sexual misadventures. I did not instigate them in many cases, but I certainly played my part. Although at times I felt intimidated and thought I was doing the wrong thing, I never once stopped an encounter from occurring and in the end became quite the player in what was to become the beginning of my sexual education, an awakening.

I kept a journal that year especially after my first encounter, as I couldn't believe it had happened at first. It was like a fantasy. The following chapters are a chronological order of events as they happened in my first year of window cleaning. That year really changed my life. I grew more confident sexually as the year went on. The older I got, the more experience I gained. An insatiable lust built up inside me over time, and it wanted to get out. I just wanted sex all the time, and I wasn't afraid to let a woman know about it. I loved to take charge of a woman and push her to the edge. As time went on, I got bolder and could never see any reason for not letting a woman know what my intentions were. Who would have thought that starting a job as a window cleaner would get me involved in as many sexual encounters as I experienced? Well, not me. Sex, sex, and more sex! I certainly got what I wished for.

I don't doubt that some reading my adventures might find them hard to believe. As I reread my journal before putting this to print, I was again surprised myself at the encounters and reexperienced in some cases the excitement and stimulation I had experienced all those years ago. Some of the encounters just seemed too unbelievable to be true. All I can say is I have no reason to lie. Today I prefer to live with the truth; I'm happier this way. So I can assure you that what I am about to share with you from my journal in 1985 will be the truth, the whole truth, and nothing but the truth, at least from my viewpoint. It's kind of like a confessional for me. It feels good to get it out.

For legal reasons I've been advised that I shouldn't mention names, businesses and so on. I have changed them for everyone's well-being and peace of mind. My name is Richard Pane! —as in windowpane—or Dick Pane for short. For the purposes of the following, you will understand why the more you read.

So anyway, as I like to tell the ladies at times, grab on to your ankles, darling. I am going downtown. This is my story to the world. Take it or leave it, and let the madness begin.

IT BEGINS

I was twenty-one years old and had been working as a labourer for a builder for the last two years. I had also been playing football for two years at a professional football club, so I was in very good condition physically. Tall, standing six feet with long dark hair and built like a statue, strong and chiselled, I was in the prime of my life, a young bull in fact. Young, dumb, and full of cum, some would say, and I could rarely think of anything else. If I wasn't sleeping, I was up for some pussy. If I couldn't get it, I would eventually have to bat it off. I was permanently horny, and masturbation was somewhat of a daily ritual if I couldn't get my fix.

The labouring job involved many hours working under houses. It was extremely hard work and involved crawling in the dirt digging holes for hours on end. The pay was good, but the work was shit. One day while driving home in busy traffic I noticed a couple of guys cleaning shop windows. The sun was shining, and they looked like they were having a ball. I could hear them laugh as I was stuck in the traffic. It sounds crazy as I write it, but I decided right then that I was going to become a window cleaner.

That weekend I bought the local newspaper. It had a Situations Vacant section on a Saturday, so I thought I would check out if there were any window-cleaning positions available. There it was: "Window Cleaner Wanted, No Experience Necessary, Will Train the Right Applicant. Call Acme Window Cleaning." Well, I didn't muck around; I gave the number a call and got an interview. At the interview I was pleasantly surprised to find out that the hours were quite short and that there were financial bonuses to be had. Basically, the more you produced, the more you got paid, not an hourly rate. This sounded great, and I was given a trial day to get a feel for the job. The boss put me up a ladder to see if I could handle heights and showed me how to use a squeegee. It all went well, and I was officially on board. I broke the news to my building boss, and I was no longer going to be crawling around in the dirt.

My first day I was nervous as any new person is. The company had about a dozen window cleaners and the boss who ran the business from an office in his home. We would all meet at around 7:15 a.m. outside his house on a suburban street, leaving our cars parked for the day while going off in company vehicles. We mostly worked in pairs, and I remember my first day and the driver showing me the ropes. The driver of the vehicle was the senior man and in charge of the crew whether it be two or three men. That first day we cleaned a lot of retail shops on the streets, and after that we cleaned a house. We finished up around 1:00 p.m., and that was it. I got to say I liked the hours, I liked the work, and compared to what I'd been doing for the previous two years, this was a breeze.

The next day it ran similar. I was with a different guy, and I tried to keep up. Over the next couple of weeks, it was a very steep learning curve. These guys worked fast. In fact, that is what this whole business seemed to be about. Get in and out as quickly as possible, and get the jobs done so you could call it a day. Some days the different crews would race each other to finish their jobs and get to the pub. It was a fast-paced, energetic workplace, no matter how you looked at it, and it was fun. There was a lot of comradery within the group. To my surprise, I was really enjoying my new career and after about three months felt that I was as good and fast a window cleaner as anyone else there.

The company had a lot of work. As well as retail shops and commercial jobs, we did lots of houses, usually when the wife was home alone during the day. I had heard a few stories from the boys about different guys who worked there and encounters they had. At first I didn't really believe them and didn't take too much notice as I thought it was just bullshit. What happened to me not long after would change all that.

"I WANT YOU TO SHOW ME YOUR COCK"

January 1985
Ronica (Roni), a work-from-home housewife

I had been working with Bob on this day, and when we arrived back at the boss's house, Bob headed off on his motorcycle. He was the senior man but wanted to get away in a hurry, so he asked if I could take the job sheet into the boss. It was no problem to me. It was only midday, and I didn't have any plans, so I headed into the office.

The boss was a nice friendly guy, always happy but also very business-orientated. He didn't tolerate any bullshit, and that was a good effort, I thought, because he was only a small guy, a gentleman really, in comparison to the guys who worked there. Most of the guys working there were bordering on psychotic. Most of them were dope-smoking, beer-drinking yobos that drove V8s and had tattoos and mullets. It was a rough crew, but the boss kept them in check mainly because they were well paid and the supervisors handled any bullshit. Most of them couldn't have found a better gig than window cleaning; believe it or not, the pay is very good if you're good at it.

Anyway, I went into the office and handed the boss the job sheet. He was on the phone, so I turned to walk away when he said, "Hang on a minute. I got another job for you." I didn't mind. Like I said, it was only midday, and I had nothing on. Also, any bonus work paid two thirds of what you made, so it was all going to be good for me. I waited until he finished his call. Before he hung up, I couldn't help but hear the conversation and noticed that he said, "Oh yes, I have just the guy. He is very strong and handsome." He then hung up looked at me and said, "Ready to do another job?"

I said, "Why not!" I was still in the early impress-the-boss stage of my career.

He laughed and said, "You should have fun. She wants someone strong and handsome!"

"Okay," I said, "that's me." I laughed, not thinking anything of it. I got the details and headed off.

This was the first time I was going out on my own, and I was a little excited, to tell the truth. I was feeling good about it really, as I had learned the ropes well, I felt. I was confident I could handle anything that was thrown my way. Boy, was I in for a surprise. On the drive over to this house, I recalled the boss saying she seemed more interested in a handsome young man than in having her windows cleaned, but the thought didn't linger or carry any more significance, as I was just excited to be doing my first job alone. The thought that I got to set the price and take two thirds of the money was exciting; I was really enjoying the freedom of my new job and the independence and control it offered.

I arrived at the house at around 1:00 p.m. It was a double-story house in a wealthy inner eastern suburb. When the door opened, an attractive older woman greeted me quite excitedly. She was probably in her forties. Her name was Ronica. I introduced myself as Dick. She smiled big at that, looking me up and down very suggestively, and said, "Come in. Dick, mm-hmm. You can call me Roni." I then interrupted her and said that I would walk around the outside of the house first and give her a quote. This was the standard procedure, so it just sort of automatically came out of my mouth. The way Roni had looked me up and down had surprised me a bit and thrown me out.

I just said, "I will be back in a minute and tell you how much it will cost."

She said, "Okay, I'll wait."

I moved around the outside of the house quickly and was soon back to inform Roni that the price would be a hundred and eighty dollars. She looked at me with a cute smile and said, "Go ahead. Just knock on the door when you're done." Not thinking anything more of it, I got stuck into the job.

I was just doing the outside and was really flying through it when I realised that this job was only going to take about an hour. I thought to myself, I should probably slow down a bit, as I didn't want her to think

I was overcharging her. It wasn't a minute later that she came out the back door and asked if I would like a cup of tea. I said, "Sure that sounds great," thinking it would eat up a bit of time. It was also then that I noticed how attractive Roni was. She was wearing a light blue top that buttoned at the front, hiding a pair of bulging breasts pressing tightly against her top and showing off a beautiful cleavage. She had on a short, skin-coloured skirt with stockings and heels. She was hot! I also now noticed how horny I was and started to think to myself and imagine fucking her. Seeing her tits pressing so tightly in her top and her tiny little arse got my motor running. It also seemed she liked me. She was flirty, smiling, giggling, wiggling, and bending her body suggestively. I thought, *Oh well, this is cool. I get to perve on this hottie while cleaning her windows, and I'm getting paid for it. Shit hot! I love this job.* About five minutes later Roni called out to me to take a break and invited me inside.

I put down my gear, took off my work belt, and went inside. Roni had set up a teapot and biscuits on a table. It all looked a bit formal, something I wasn't really used to. She told me to take a seat and relax. She said she had been watching how hard I was working and wanted me to relax for a while. It was at that moment that I noticed she seemed to be slightly slurring or a bit drunk maybe. I don't know. But wow, she was a beautiful woman. I could feel myself getting excited and my heartbeat increasing just like whenever I'm going after a woman and there is a chance of sex. I sat at the table and noticed I was getting aroused, as I had the beginnings of a chubby in my shorts. I made a slight adjustment to accommodate this as discreetly as I could. She poured me a cup of tea from the pot, very elegantly. Roni was a real lady and moved very sensually, not like most girls I had been with. I was trying to keep it together and be cool, and then her phone rang. She headed for a glass table the phone was on and sat on a chair and took the call. She was just so sexy; I was really starting to notice how hot she was and how turned on I was getting. Also, now with her on the phone distracted, I could really have a good look at her without her noticing—or so I thought. She sat so fine on the chair, perfect posture, legs crossed and rubbing her calf while engaged in the call. I had a good look at her while she wasn't looking and gulped down my tea. She was fucking hot, and I would totally have loved to fuck her, but I had no idea where to begin. While sitting on the chair, her tight little miniskirt had almost turned into a belt it had ridden up so high. She was much more mature than any woman I had ever been interested in, and I was becoming quite flustered. My penis stirred, and there wasn't much room in my footy shorts once things heated up. She finished her call, and I busied myself in eating the biscuit and sipping tea, trying to look like I hadn't been perving.

"Sorry about that," she said. "I work from home. I'm on the phone a lot. How's the tea?"

I thought to myself, *Is she fucking with me? This is one of the greatest cups of tea I've ever had.* "It's great," I said nervously. Roni was now sitting directly in front of me. Her hands were on her knees, and I could see straight up her skirt. She was beautiful, petite, and big-breasted, and it looked like to me that she had no knickers on. I tried to not make it too obvious, but I blew it, and she caught me looking. Embarrassed, I stood up quickly, adjusting my cock as I did, as it had firmed and was hard to hide. I started to thank her for the cuppa, and she crossed her legs and leaned back in her chair, twirling her hair. I could still see straight up her skirt. Her knickers were visible; actually, I couldn't tell if she had any or not. She was now looking at me like she knew I was into her. She had caught me perving, but how could I not? She was smoking hot, and that skirt was so short, like it had hiked right higher than it should have been. It was very distracting, and my eyes kept looking down there.

Roni was also glancing down noticeably at the bulge in my shorts, which had been getting larger and obvious, and she was really looking at me suggestively. After what seemed like such an awkward minute, Roni stood up and said, "Well, you had better get back to it," and I turned and went out the door.

Wow! I had never had such an intense, nerve-racking, and erotic experience ever. She was into me? Or was she just teasing me? I had no idea, and I really was still very immature when it came to women. All I knew is that I would love to fuck her and fuck her hard. I squeezed my cock when I knew she couldn't see me. I was pumped up and knew I could shoot a load quite quickly. I thought to myself, *I've got to get this job finished and get out of here, so I can get home and wank it off.* It took me another fifteen minutes to finish the job, then

I went out to the van for about another ten minutes, pretending to pack up. I tried calming myself down as I was in quite a funk before going back to the front door to let Roni know I was done. I was looking forward to having one last look at Roni. She was seriously sexy and definitely giving me more than the usual woman does, and I was loving it, even as flustered as I was. At the same time I was nervous, as it just felt so wrong that I would be getting it on with a customer on the job. Surely this was never going to happen.

I planned to just say I was done and that we'd send her an invoice. Sometimes we got paid cash; other times we just invoiced, but I just wanted to get out of there as quickly as possible as I was as horny as fuck and needed to release. I thought this would have been the quickest way, but to my surprise Roni wasn't finished with me yet. I had no idea. She opened the door, and I started to tell her I was done when she interrupted and said she would like to make sure I had gotten everything. She invited me in and said she would be back in a moment. I waited nervously for a couple of minutes in the entry. On returning she complimented me on my excellent job; she was very happy. She was prancing around and really turning it on. She started touching my arms and shoulder, even stroking me while thanking me for the excellent job. I told her awkwardly it was my pleasure as it certainly had been. As I started to turn to leave, she said, "There's just one last thing I would like."

The way she said it, the tone and suggestion in her voice, was so suggestive I could feel my cock stirring. I was shaking, and I had to get away from this lady. I was freaking out! I stopped, turned and nervously, and said, "Yeah, sure."

She said, "I would like to see your cock."

I laughed shyly at first, not really realising, and said, "Yeah, what?"

She said, "I want you to show me your cock." She leaned forward and grabbed my cock. I sort of moved away, acting as if I was shocked, but I loved it. I was a bit confused. I probably looked like a deer in the spotlight. I was thinking, *What? What are you talking about?* Roni grabbed my hand and hauled me inside, shutting the door.

She then whispered in my ear, "I want to see your cock, and I want to make you cum!" I was dumbfounded. She led me by the hand back to the tea table. She sat down on her phone chair and asked me if I thought she was sexy.

I was speechless. "Of course," I think I said. "You're beautiful." Looking up at me and touching herself, she told me again she wanted to see my cock. At this stage I was ready to explode. I was so fucking horny. Nothing like this had ever even remotely happened to me, and I was a mess. She sat in front of me, staring at my shorts, and started to feel my bulging cock through my shorts. She was purring, and I was stiffening quickly.

She asked me, "Are you going to get it out, or can I?"

I just mumbled, "Yeah, I guess," while struggling to breathe. I was just too overwhelmed to pull out my cock. I was stunned. My cock was so hard by now, pressing uncomfortably in my footy shorts. I was literally busting out of my shorts, and it hadn't gone unnoticed by Roni. She pulled her phone chair over more closely in front of me and sat down, spreading her legs wide apart. She pressed her face softly against my bulging shorts. I could finally tell for sure she did have knickers on. They were just so fine that you could see right through them, and her hand was going at it too. She was fingering herself. She had taken only moments to get at herself, and she was on display. She was in her own world. I thought for a moment that it wouldn't even matter if I were there or not. But I was there, and, fuck, this was as sexy a misadventure as I had ever experienced, and I totally lost control.

While Roni was going at it, moaning softly at first but increasing her panting quickly, I just stood there so turned on I thought I was going to cum in my shorts. I was lucky I was wearing football shorts as they had a fair bit of stretch. My cock was angled to the left and up, hard as a rock, as she'd been rubbing it very nicely with one hand and nibbling it through my shorts. Her other hand was playing with herself, and her moaning was a real turn-on. I needed relief so badly it was pressing up uncomfortably, so I just undid and pulled my shorts down, releasing the pressure. My cock sprang out right in front of her face, big, hard, and bulging. Roni screamed with delight at the sight of this and immediately started to admire my full erection. Roni was amazing. She was really impressed by my cock and enjoying it, as was I. It was like it was a piece of fine art or a rare museum piece the way she admired it. It wasn't often a beautiful woman would have my cock this hard and just admire it; in fact, this had never happened before. She commented that I had a beautiful cock and that it looked like I was ready to cum. *No kidding*, I thought. I was so hot to burst just her touching it for a little longer and I'd be done. I was dribbling precum like crazy, sticky, and she started to play with it in her fingers and rubbed the head of my cock. She had also been pleasuring herself while all this was happening and was now really giving herself a good go, moaning loudly and really getting off. I'd never experienced anything quite like it. I was just standing there, but my cock was hard and wanting to burst. She began to kiss my cock softly at first and then, mouth open, just gaping, she started to suck on it hard.

I'd never experienced a sensation quite like this. The first couple of sucks were incredible, the sensation a feeling of ecstasy. I looked down at this amazingly sensual woman, and my heart was racing. I was red-faced and anxious as hell, I didn't know what to do. Suddenly Roni opened her eyes and looked at me so wantonly I lost control. I was never in control. She started to suck on my cock fully and deeply, the likes of which I had never had before. I was so hard now, though, and nothing could stop me. I forced it right in Roni's mouth all the way to the hilt, and she gagged. It just happened; I couldn't even control myself, and it seemed like she was in total agreement. I drove it in so deep and thrust in and out like I was fucking her face while clasping the back of her head. I pounded her face so hard a couple of times it sounded like I was chocking her, and in fact I was. She was gagging and gasping, and then I released the mightiest orgasm of my life. I roared while holding her head tightly to my body, releasing my entire load down her throat and gyrating, violently thrusting a couple of times as I finished. It was so intense I roared out loud like I had never done before.

Roni gasped loudly as I released her and my full cock left her mouth. I had really rammed it in there. I fell back on the single seater couch, shorts down around my ankles. I was spent. I lay there breathing heavily for a minute as my attention started to turn to Roni. She was lying on the floor. I had pumped her face so hard she was laying back, looking almost like she was dead, except I could see her breathing heavily. It looked as if someone had assaulted her. Her clothes were dishevelled, and she looked like she'd been crying. I was spent myself but quickly regained my composure when I thought she was hurt. I pulled up my shorts, packing my still-swollen cock away as best I could, and grabbed her by the shoulders. She took a deep breath while getting herself off the floor, sighed, licked her lips, and said, "Wow you're a naughty boy!" She started to put herself back together and then offered me another cup of tea. I was in shock. What had just happened? The most erotic misadventure of my life, that's what. I told Roni that I really had to go now, and I really felt like I had done something wrong and I was sorry. She nonchalantly walked to another room and said she would expect more next time and hoped I would be able to deliver. She would talk to the office about her next service.

With that I thanked her and told her I had to go and left. I mean, I thanked her. I couldn't believe I just thanked a lady I felt like I had just raped—or did she rape me? I mean, she started it. Well, that's what I thought. I was fucking confused, and I had no idea what was going to happen when the boss found out. I was a mess. I had never done that to a woman before. I just fucked her face so furiously, I totally lost control. I felt like I had raped her, but she did kind of ask for it. The sex I was normally used to was never like that. In fact, that was the first time I had ever really cum in a woman's mouth. Well, there had been some other occasions, but nothing like that. My cock had been so deep down her throat it felt like I'd cum directly in her stomach. It was also the best orgasm I had ever experienced. So wild and raw it was electrifying. I felt amazing.

I drove back to the boss's house, parked the car, and headed home. I didn't go and see the boss as I was shitting myself. I had messed up badly. I had a girlfriend and everything, not that I ever let that stop me. If I could get sex with someone, then I'd fuck. Fuck, I couldn't tell her either; I couldn't tell anyone. I was in a real funk.

At home that night I couldn't believe what had happened. I was kind of in shock, an erotic shock where you have had this amazing experience, but you think you're about to get hung for it. I mean, I knew she came on to me; she wanted me to show her my cock, which was cool, I thought, but she didn't ask for anything else, and I had certainly lost control. I didn't know if there

Richard Pane

would be any consequences for that, as I had never done anything like this in my life, certainly not with a stranger. Most of my sexual experiences up until that point had been lame by comparison, standard stuff, not choking a middle-aged woman with my cock in her lounge room in the middle of the day. I also couldn't help but wonder whether it was good for Roni. I got my rocks off. It was awesome, best climax I had ever had, but could it really feel good for a woman to have her face fucked like that? Choking on a cock? I was a bit of a mess and nervous about work the following day, wondering whether I would be sacked, arrested, or both. I would have to wait and see.

THE NEXT DAY

I arrived in the street at 7:15 a.m. We start at 7:30, but it was always good to get there a bit early to have a chat catch up with the guys, etc. The boss usually came out around 7:25 to give out the job sheets for the day. When he comes out, he usually just hands the little clipboards to the drivers with their respective job sheets. Everyone would be keen to see whom they were working with and what sort of day they had ahead of them. I just stood back and waited to try to hide and not be noticed. I was still totally freaked out from the day before and waiting and looking for any signs I was in the shit.

It was Friday, and a few of the guys were talking about the weekend and what they were getting up to. That's when it happened. The boss asked me how long

16

that house took me yesterday. I was speechless, and my heart froze as I thought, *This is it.*

He then said, "I didn't see you when you came back. Next time make sure you drop the job sheet back to the office. I had to call the lady to find out what went on."

I nervously said, "Okay."

He said, "One hundred and eight dollars for a two-hour job? That's pretty good. Well done, nice bit of bonus."

The other guys suddenly waded in. "Jeez, that's great," said Wayne.

"You're an animal" said Peter, and Andrew one of the most senior guys just looked at me and smiled.

"You're learning."

All the guys there had been responsible for training me. That's how it was at Acme Window Cleaning; you learned on the job, and I had been out with them all over the last three months. The boss then said, "Well, she was very happy with you, told me you did an excellent job, and she wants you back again."

"Woo-hoo," said the guys in chorus with a bit of laughter.

"I bet she does," said Wayne.

"As a matter of fact, you'll have to go by there today as you left an extension pole, and she doesn't want it lying around, so go back and get it okay? I told her you would."

The guys burst into laughter with that one: he left an extension pole, ha-ha. It was quite funny but was doing nothing for my mental state. I was in a fizz, but it seemed like all was okay. With that everyone started heading to the vehicles and getting set up for the day. I was still stunned.

I was working with Wayne, and as we started to head of I thought, *Jeez, I can't believe it, I was a nervous wreck and for nothing.* Everything seemed okay. Roni was happy! The boss was happy! I was suddenly very relieved and happy. Shit, what an amazing experience, and it wasn't over yet. I had to go back to pick up the extension pole I had left. Funny really, Roni had certainly given me an extension pole. A big fat dribbling one that I'd shot down her throat, I thought with a grin. I'm not surprised I left without it. With all that was going on, I'm surprised I didn't just hand myself in to the authorities. The experience with Roni had well and truly rocked me, and the thought of seeing her again so soon was both nerve-racking and stimulating. She was after all hot, and she had just let me do what I did to her, so who knew where this adventure would end up. One thing I knew was I loved having sex, and I really enjoyed new encounters. I was interested to see what happened next.

Wayne was an experienced hand at the company and had been there for years. He was one of the three supervisors. He had tattoos, dark hair, a mullet, a moustache, and a goatee, and by my estimation he was a bloody tough bugger. He didn't like the boss, but not many did. They all bitched about him, but he did like the money in window cleaning and that's what kept him there. We got on very well, and I liked him. He seemed to enjoy my company also and we worked well together. We had some shops to do and then we got something to eat. That was the usual routine. As we were pigging out in the car, he suggested we could pick up the extension pole from Roni's next as it was nearby and on the way to a block of flats we had next.

I told him, "That's okay. I can go and pick it up later after we knock off. I don't want to waste your time." The truth was I didn't want anyone finding out about what had happened as I was still shit scared and a bit embarrassed to let anyone know. I felt vulnerable, like I could be in trouble, and I just didn't want anybody to know.

Wayne was having none of that and said, "We'll just go and get it and be done with it."

I said okay as I didn't want to make a bigger deal of it. We finished our break and headed to Roni's. My heart was pumping now. We pulled up at her house and Wayne said, "Well, go get it, bozo."

I got out of the car. Unfortunately Wayne had parked us directly opposite Roni's front door. It was a warm day, so his window was down, and he was likely going to hear everything Roni had to say. Fuck! I was nervous. I was going to have to be quick, just get the pole and get out of there. But, shit, I wanted to talk to her. I mean, all I had really done was fuck her throat, and I felt a little embarrassed and guilty that I hadn't given her a more loving romantic experience. Isn't that what women want? I thought. What was I thinking about? Jeez, what a predicament. As I approached the door, I suddenly thought maybe I could just jump the fence and grab it and leave, so I started looking over the fence to where I thought it was. Wayne saw me and screamed out, "Stop fucking around and just get it. We've got get going."

Damn it! I was going to have to knock on the door, so I took a deep breath and knocked. Roni opened the door with that same beautiful flirtatious smile I had seen the day before. She asked me in. I hesitated and said, "I really can't. I'm with another guy today working, and we need to get going." I turned and motioned toward the car. Wayne was smoking a cigarette and looking mean as usual.

Roni said, "Well, you'll have to come inside to get your pole thingy. I'm not touching that dirty thing." Her tone was so suggestive it took me straight back to yesterday, and I felt a tingling and stiffening in my shorts. I entered the house, and she shut the door. We were face to face again. She launched herself on me. I grabbed her tightly to match her as our mouths locked and our tongues danced vigorously. We hadn't kissed until now, and it was a passionate release. We really fitted well together. I grabbed her arse and really had a good feel of her as I hadn't the opportunity until now. We were into each other; I was already hardening and bursting out of my shorts again when I realised I had to stop.

I shouted, "Fuck, I've got to go. Can we catch up later? Wayne's outside, and we've got work to do. I can come around after that." I was nodding and waiting for a reaction from her. Jeez, I was a mess. She smiled and kissed me softly while grabbing my cock. That wasn't going to help me get to the car any faster. "Shit, let me get the pole and I'll come back about two p.m."

Roni stepped away and smiled. She didn't have a care in the world. "I'll be waiting," she said. I turned and headed out to the backyard, grabbed the extension pole, and headed back through the house to the front door. I paused for a minute, and we both laughed as I waited for my erection to go down—not easy with her standing right there. Her beauty and smell were intoxicating. I repositioned myself in my shorts, opened the door, and left walking swiftly to the rear of the van to put the pole away. I again adjusted my own pole, got in, and we were on our way.

We got to the block of flats and did the usual thing of drive around first and look at what we could get away with. This was standard procedure at the company, as the boss would always say, "We don't clean a clean window." With that as a motto, I can assure you the guys took it to the limit. Half an hour and we were done and then we headed for a house. It was a big one in a wealthy suburb. There was already another crew there working inside, so we just started on the outside, and within an hour we were done. It was 12:30 p.m. by the time we left the house and headed back to the office. We parked the car, cleaned it out, put the rags in the wash, and headed to the office. Once the job sheet was handed over to the boss and the what's-on-the-weekend talk was out of the way, we headed out.

Wayne was in a relationship, not married but the kind of relationship that was like a marriage. Committed and together, they sounded like they had similar goals and were right for each other. He still liked to look at the pretty girls but would never take it any further—or so he said. I, however, was something else. I had been having sex with anyone since I was seventeen, although my first encounter was with a prostitute, paid for by a mate who had just returned from his basic training in the army. He didn't realise it was my first time, and I was too shy to tell anyone. Not long after that I started to go to bars, clubs, discos, seeing bands, etc. And of course there were always girls. I liked getting with a stranger if she was pretty enough and having sex. I loved a one-night stand and the quick get-down-and-dirty of it all. I would usually just get hard, and after a bit of a pash and chew on the tits, hands groping everywhere, I'd just put it in and pump as fast and hard as I could until I'd cum. With some girls you'd hang around for a couple of goes at it during the night, but with others I'd just be on my way. The only problem with them, though, was that they would sometimes turn into more than a one-night, and a girl can get jealous. Not always, but when you're as active as I was back then, something's going to happen. I didn't care when or where, but whenever my mates and I went out, we wanted to score and to me that meant sex. Sex became my drug, and I never seemed to get enough. I was, however, currently in a relationship. I had been seeing a girl who was my girlfriend for about two years. We would spend a lot of nights together even though I didn't live with her. She lived with three others, a little older women. She was the baby, or that's how they treated her. I would stay at her house a couple of nights a week, and she would come over to mine occasionally. Usually on Thursday nights we wouldn't see each other because I had footy training and then would go out with the boys, get pissed, and try and score. However, I was in such a funk the night before that I hadn't gone out after training, just headed home to await my fate. Friday nights my girlfriend and I always got together and hung out as it was the end of the work week, usually watching a movie and just chilling.

Anyway, on this day, it was only about 2:00 p.m., and I was off to see Roni. I would catch up with my girlfriend later, I thought. What I had ahead of me was just too exciting.

On arriving at Roni's, I knocked on her door and waited a minute. I was still really anxious because even though we kind of broke the ice this morning, I still hadn't even really talked to this woman, and she was so stunning I wasn't sure I could be comfortable without being a jabbering mess. When she opened the door, I felt my cock instantly stir with anticipation. It was like the brain had just opened the flow of blood to my dick. She smiled and motioned me in, shutting the door. She gave me a gentle kiss and caress, purring a little. She really liked me. She offered a cup of tea, which I accepted, and I stood awkwardly in her kitchen while she turned on the kettle and got out some cups. "Take a seat I'll be with you in a minute," she said, motioning me to the couch, the scene of the crime.

I wandered in, looking around not sitting. I was very much on edge still, not feeling at home or myself around Roni. This woman really intimidated me. It was her beauty, maturity, and raw sexuality. I think also because most of my previous sexual encounters had been drunken one-nighters or with my girlfriend. This situation with Roni was completely different. It was mid-afternoon on a Friday in a posh lady's home, and I hadn't had a drink. She was a real woman as well more mature, and as I was slowly realising I had not been with one before in my life. Any sex I had had before Roni was with young immature girls, not really women. I was immature myself, and this was something different. I could feel it and I was not yet comfortable. She came in with the tea on a tray and placed it on the coffee table, telling me to sit once more, and this time I did. She poured the tea and gave it to me with a couple of biscuits. She poured one for herself and then sat ninety degrees from me, looking very relaxed. I was speechless and blushing but managed to thank her for the tea. She said it was her pleasure but hoped we could make it to the bedroom this time.

Jeez, she didn't muck around. My cock firmed some more. She was a stunning woman and now I told her so. "You're beautiful Roni." She smiled and thanked me.

"Do you like my outfit?" She was wearing a white shapely top with a brown pleated skirt and pink heels and stockings. She looked sexy. I told her I liked her outfit, especially the heels and stockings, and that she was very sexy. "So, you like stockings?" Standing up, she lifted her skirt to reveal she didn't have any undies on, just these sexy as garter belts and the stockings. I could see the black of her bush but below all naked and ready. She started to give me a bit of a show, stretching, posing, and rolling around on the couch before she said, "Come with me."

I was full on tent-pole hard by now and just released my cock from my shorts by stretching my shorts leg up because it was uncomfortable, and she was going to get it. I followed her to the bedroom, my cock swinging as I walked, but it was so hard nothing could stop it. She had a big bedroom with a king-size bed. I grabbed her and turned her around, kissing her vigorously, my cock pressing against her tummy, with only her clothes separating our flesh. Within a minute our clothes were completely off except for those sexy little stockings, and I was inside her, driving my cock in and out with such ferocity it was intense. Her legs spread wide, I pumped her for a while, probably only a minute, but it felt like a good serve, then grabbed her ankles and pressed them back by her ears. She was flexible. It made for maximum penetration, and I pounded her hard, a real collision of pelvises, over and over. Before I knew it I was cuming. So loud, so energetic, I roared again like the day before. I just couldn't control myself once I got a pumping. I don't think I have cum so vigorously before, except maybe the day before perhaps. This one was different, though. I was fucking her, and I loved it—fucking her and fucking her hard.

Lying there recovering I realised I had again cum very quickly. She had this kind of effect on me. In fact that's how I always fucked—the original fast and furious. Embarrassed!

"Was that good for you," I asked.

She was on her side rubbing my chest, her leg rubbing over my cock. "Oh yeah, but I could have some more. What else can you do?" she asked suggestively.

I didn't really know what else there was, so I said, "How about doggie?" She laughed! I mean really laughed, kind of uncontrollably, and I got a bit embarrassed.

She could tell I think and said, "Let's go and have a shower." I followed her to the bathroom. It was huge also. We had a shower together, kissing, caressing, and rubbing each other's bits until I was ready to go again. We dried off with her nice towels and then she dropped to her knees and started to suck my cock, savouring it lovingly like nothing I had ever experienced. She pulled it, licked, and sucked my balls, both hands in play, with the occasional deep-throat action like the day before. It was incredible. I was really enjoying it and heading toward climax again when she stopped and said. "Let's go back to the bed."

It was then Roni said, "That's what I want you to do for me."

"What, suck your cock?" I had no idea what she meant at first and then I got it. She lay down, spreading her legs wide and offering me her pussy. I had never really gone down on a woman before. I had heard of it, but I always had the idea it was kind of disgusting! I mean, that's where I put my cock, and I cum in there, so I'm not going to lick it. I didn't want to taste my own cum. Gross! Also, you piss out of there. But we'd just had a shower, and with Roni it just seemed right. I felt like I was made for it. I started to climb on top, cock hard and aching to get back inside her, especially after her sucking. I hesitated, though, and started to kiss her tits. They were a beautiful size for her petite body, and I savoured them, licking, kissing, and sucking her nipples while she moaned. Oh I loved playing with them. I moved down her body, kissing and licking, exploring her like I had never done with any woman before. There was something about her that made me want to do this.

When I eventually arrived at her pussy, although bushy at the front, it was trim where it counted, and I kissed it, slowly at first, increasing in pressure until I started to lick. It felt so amazing, so soft, like I was kissing her lips. It just sort of came naturally to me; I didn't really know what I was doing, but whatever it was she was loving it, and so was I. The more I licked and sucked at her bits, the more she moaned and orgasmed. I'd never really been able to tell when a woman was cuming before. For sure, I mean they made some noise, but it never seemed as definitive as me cuming. I mean, when I cum, you know, it spurts everywhere and then I'm done, at least for a time. Well, the more I sucked on Roni, the more she moaned and screamed. A couple of times I stopped to check she was all right. She was, and after what seemed like forever, probably a good half an hour, I got back on and into her and started pumping away.

All this oral sex had made me so hard and horny, and it wasn't going to be long before I was cuming again. The fact that I had come earlier did give me some more staying power, though. I pumped and pumped hard, really slapping my hips against her as I drove my cock in as deep as I could go. The slapping sound drove me on until I exploded inside her for a second time that afternoon. It was an intense fuck the likes of which I had never had. With that we both lay exhausted on her bed, breathing heavily until our heart rates subsided and we could talk again. Roni's first words were "You promised me doggie."

I laughed and said, "Yeah, I'll give it to you doggie next time."

She snuggled into me, and I must admit it felt pretty nice, but I was now thinking about leaving as I could tell it was getting late and I couldn't really tell my girlfriend I'd been shagging this hottie all afternoon and that's why I'm late home. I got up and started to get my clothes on. Roni just lay on the bed looking at me. She smiled and said, "I love your body, and you have a great arse." I thanked her. It seemed like a nice compliment. I knew women liked my body and found me attractive. I had always got a lot of attention from women, just never one as old as Roni, or so I thought—maybe I'd never noticed.

I told her she was sexy for me and that the sex with her was at another level. "I've never done what we did before," I told her.

"Well, if you want some more, you can have me anytime. Except after dark—that's when my husband comes around, but during most days I'm here if you want it, especially if you play as nice as you did today."

I was almost fully dressed and just standing there surprised. "Your husband? You mean you're married?" I said, shocked.

"Yes, I'm married." Roni laughed. "What did you think, I just live in this huge house by myself? Someone must pay for it, and pay for it he does. Anyway, when will you see me again?"

I was shocked and now wondering how quickly I could get out of there. Roni read my mind and told me not to worry; her husband was away interstate on business. "He's probably screwing some young tart. That's more his thing these days," she said. "He has nothing for me, and he can hardly get it up anyway. He goes to bed drunk every night."

This was all a bit of a surprise suddenly, a lot to take in on a Friday afternoon. I got Roni's phone number and told her I would call her Monday. I had to go now. She just smiled and thanked me for the wonderful afternoon. With that I took myself to the front door. She followed me naked and let me out, stroking my arm as I left. "Hope to see you Monday," she said.

"Goodbye." Not for the first time, Roni had freaked me out.

Wow, it was around ten past five and time to head home. The girlfriend would be expecting to go and get some dinner together and probably hire a video. Oh no, if she found out about this, we'd be finished. Fuck, I could never let her find out. The whole way home I couldn't get my mind off how intense the sex had been with Roni. It was amazing, like nothing I'd ever had before. I was lucky to ever even get my girlfriend to touch my cock, let alone suck it, especially as masterfully as Roni. It had been an exhilarating afternoon. Ahh, what a Friday it had been, the best Friday of my life.

That night I went around to the girlfriend's house, and we decided to get Chinese takeaway and rent a movie. After the movie we petted on the couch for a while and then I took her to bed and fucked her, because she wanted it. She never wanted sex as much as me, so I always obliged when she was in the mood. I was happy that night to just go to sleep, as I had already had my fill that day as you know. But whenever I had the opportunity to fuck, I fucked. It really didn't take much to get me going. Friday nights were fun with the girlfriend. We had been together for about two years, and she was my first real relationship. I loved her and enjoyed her company always. She was more outgoing and social than me. We liked to watch movies together, go out for dinner, or get takeaway. It was a cute relationship when I look back at it now. She also loved being around the football club as I was one of the young stars and she loved the attention that came with that. We were both very immature and naive in the ways of the world and in relationships. At the time I had no idea just how damaging my infidelities would be. I really didn't understand it and thought it was normal, harmless, and okay to be having extra sex with anyone I could get with. I really thought this sort of behaviour was normal, which sort of shows where I was at and that I had no idea.

The weekend was coming to an end on Sunday night, and as I left the girlfriend's house, my attention turned to Roni. I was quite invigorated just thinking about her, and the thoughts of her made me adjust myself pleasurably. I told Roni I would call her on Monday. I was still blown out that she was married. For some reason I felt like I needed to talk about this, probably just for my own self-preservation. One thing I didn't want was to be caught with my pants down by an angry husband. The idea of that really scared me.

Monday morning I arrived at work chipper as a bird. I was whistling, cracking jokes with the guys, and having the time of my life. Most of the crew had the Monday morning blues and wanted me to shut the fuck up! I was excited, though, as I couldn't wait to see what the day had in store. I was eager to call Roni as soon as possible as I was horny as hell and looking forward to fucking her. I hadn't had sex since fucking the girlfriend on Friday night, and she wouldn't want it again for a fortnight, if that. I'd spent the night before thinking about our two sexual encounters so far and couldn't wait to get into some more. I loved the feeling of entering Roni's vagina and fucking until I orgasmed. That said, I was still nervous about calling her. I hadn't called her before, and I always found calling girls or women I wanted to have sex with difficult. At least until I knew them and that they were okay with it. You knew setting up a date was nerve-racking enough, and this was like that. My plan was to wait until we finished our day and then give her a call from a phone booth. Hopefully all would be good, and I could just go over and do whatever I wanted to her. Well, that was my plan, and I was excited. I was going to get a root, and that's all that mattered.

The day went well and as planned. I worked with Bob every Monday; he was in his late thirties, married, and was a real pro. He never mucked around on the job. It was always just get in and get out, all business. He'd been working in the industry for many years and was brought over from another big company as a supervisor. He knew his craft well and didn't take any shit from the guys. We got along well, worked well together, and had a lot of laughs. He also had an eye for the ladies, so we were always checking them out and sharing tales. I had not, however, let him know about Roni, and that was difficult because we got on so well.

As usual Bob had us wrapped up at one o'clock; you could set your watch by him. I didn't stuff around either. I said my goodbyes and was out of there. By now I was in a bit of a froth and wanted to ring Roni. I wanted to know where we were at. To tell the truth I was looking forward to banging her doggie style. I loved fucking doggie style. It made for the best fuck, and with Roni, I knew it would be sweet. I'd been thinking about that and that I hadn't done it yet. I was such a simple man, but really it was all I had on my mind. I headed toward her house and stopped at the first phone booth I found. Fuck it! It was trashed. Some arsehole had ripped off the receiver. I got back in the car on my way to the next. I was about two minutes away from her house when I found another. No excuses this time. I dialled her number. She didn't answer, and it went to her answering machine. Fuck, I wasn't expecting that. I hung up. I called again. Damn it, same again. I couldn't leave a message, so I decided to wait awhile. What the fuck. Ten minutes later I called again. Still no answer. I didn't know what to do, damn it! I had my whole day planned, but I hadn't accounted for this. I thought maybe I should just go around there. So I did. I parked a little down the road and walked past her house a couple of times. Jeez, I was becoming a real freak. What had this woman done to me? I didn't know, but I wanted some more. Like a dog on heat I banged on her door. I thought, What the fuck? If hubby answered, I'd just say I got the wrong house. Well, to my relief Roni answered. She was home. It was two o'clock by now, and I was ready to give her a real pumping—at least that's what had been going through my mind. I really wanted to give it to her doggie style as we had discussed so casually on Friday. I'd been fantasising about that all weekend and couldn't wait to get back at her, and that's exactly what I did.

JOURNAL ENTRY JANUARY 24, 1985

Roni

Today I had the most amazing experience of my life. I was working at a customer's house cleaning the windows, and the customer was home alone, and she sucked me off. Her name was Roni, and she was a beautiful older sexy woman. I'm writing this record as I couldn't believe what happened, and I want a record of what happened. She started by flirting with me and inviting me in for tea. After this when I had completed the job, she just asked me if I would show her my cock. One thing led to another, and I ended up cuming down her throat after she sucked me off. It was intense. I also think I might be in trouble.

FROM THEN ON

I first met Roni in late January 1985. Roni was gorgeous, petite, sexy, and always wore sexy stockings, pantyhose, and heels. She was a well-kept woman. I fucked her about a couple of dozen times. She was in her early forties, I estimated and up until that time the oldest and most experienced woman I had ever been with.

After our first encounter I got together with her always at her home in the afternoons. Eventually I had to stop seeing her, as her husband had grown suspicious, or at least that's what she said. Sex with her was amazing, and she taught me a lot. Everything really. She was the beginning of my sexual maturity, at least in the art of making a woman cum. She used to make me chew her through her pantyhose, driving her and me wild until I would eventually rip a hole in her hose. I would spend a lot of time eating her out, then I would fuck her furiously. She would climax repeatedly and want at it again and again. I don't remember making a woman climax before her as she taught me to really pleasure a woman. Her pure sexuality would force me to spend more time devouring every inch of her body. Her pleasurable moans guided my mouth and opened the door to my potential. I would kiss and suck and lick her out for ages, both her pussy and, surprisingly for me, her arsehole. I had never done anything like this before. I was also becoming a lot more in control of my own climaxes. I was able to fuck for longer and control my finishes. It was great.

I stopped seeing her after a couple of months. Like she said: her husband had grown suspect.

Later that year in August she did get her windows done again. I fucked her while Andrew did the windows on the outside while I was on the inside. Wink, wink! It was great to get back in her. We got together for about another month, meeting weekly, and then I never saw her again. I still remember the last time I fucked her. We did it standing up doggie style, her hands against the wall while I pumped in and out hard with my hands around her neck, choking her. I would bang her like crazy. She was such a great fuck, and I had come a long way sexually. It was spectacular. She loved everything we did together, and so did I.

"GO AND TAKE A SHOWER, AND I'LL GIVE YOU A BLOWJOB"

February 1985
Kim the Receptionist

I first got with Kim in early February. Kim was a receptionist at an engineering company. She was in her early forties. We used to clean the front office windows weekly. She was stunning; all the guys used to talk about her. She was literally sex on a stick is what I'd call her. Reason being that when you saw her, that was all you could think about: sex. Other women hated her as she was that stunningly sexual. They were intimidated and jealous. She was about five feet ten inches tall, slim, with nice-size tits and a smoking hot arse, legs that were perfect, beautifully tanned skin, and dark long brunette hair. She was always made up stunningly, with long eyelashes and red lips, and she wore the shortest, tightest skirts, biggest heels, and stockings with a garter. Fucking crazy. She reminded me of Tarzan's Jane in a way, a wild and sexy beast. The best thing about this job was when we were done with the window cleaning, we would have to collect the cash. We would always go in together and make some small talk if possible, if there was no one else there. She would then have to get up out of her seat and get cash from the other end of reception. You would always get to perve at her then. I would see her panties every time we did the windows as she wore the shortest skirts. She knew it too, and I thought she had her eye on me from the start. Truth was she loved the attention and probably got lots of cock. I just never thought I'd get her too.

One time after doing the windows I left a note on her car window. Bob had dared me to. It said, "I love you," but I drew an eye, a love heart, and a big letter U. Pretty sick, hey. And I wrote my phone number. I remember thinking this was romantic, and I had had a friend who used this approach with success, so what the heck. I was nervous as hell but thought there was nothing really to lose. I waited all day, anxiously awaiting her call as surely the note created a bit of a mystery. The unknowns from my perspective were: Does she have a boyfriend? Is she married? Both were highly likely as she was stunning. And then I was also nervous because I was in a relationship and shouldn't have been doing this.

She called at the end of the day and said, "Oh, it's you! I wasn't sure who left the note."

To my surprise she agreed to meet me at a beach-side hotel the next day after work for a drink. I was kind of nervous as I was meeting her at a hotel not too far from where I lived. I was worried I might be seen and get busted by someone I knew, but this woman was so hot I wasn't going to say no. Also I was just anxious about how this would go as it was really outside my normal approaches to women. But let me tell you Kim was worth the approach.

When she arrived at the hotel, I couldn't believe my luck as I really wasn't sure she would show up. Bob was certain; he could tell, he said. I've still got to thank him to this day. We chatted, making small talk at first and had a couple of drinks. I got the first round. Kim was having lemon and vodka and mentioned that a couple of them always made her horny. I was very surprised and happy to hear this but played it cool and told her how beautiful she was. She almost seemed embarrassed with my compliment, and she reached out and touched me on the leg. The more we chatted, the touchier Kim became. This date was progressing very well. At this point I asked her if she had a boyfriend, and she told me she did. Fuck it, I thought. "Why are you here then?" I asked.

She told me she was curious from the note and found me attractive. This was great to hear.

"But what about the boyfriend?" I asked.

Kim got up to get the next round of drinks, and I noticed that other people in the bar were looking at Kim, both men and women. She was that stunningly sexual. I saw a guy I knew while there, but I don't think he noticed me, but I caught him looking at Kim. After two drinks Kim said she'd had enough, and she invited me back to her flat. She said any more drinks and she'd lose control, and she was enjoying my company and lived alone. I was so excited! But I acted cool. Kim said she and her boyfriend had been arguing lately and had broken up and that he wasn't much of a boyfriend anyway. I was keen as hell to go back to her flat. This was how every one-night stand had always played out in the past. I followed her in my car, and I didn't know what was going to happen. I was just wrapped and excited that things had progressed so fast. One minute I was waiting alone at the pub, unsure whether she would come, and now I was heading back to her place after a couple of drinks, and she had been very touchy. It was crazy how fast this was progressing. I didn't even know this girl, nor she me. *Oh well, just roll with it*, I thought. *What's the worst that could happen? The boyfriend?*

I was anxious as I entered her flat, buzzing with the alcohol and anticipation of the unknown. I sat on her couch uncomfortably as I was still partly in my work gear—footy shorts, and a fresh polo shirt—and a bit dirty from a day's work. Her couch was nice white leather, and I was worried I might dirty it. I was just nervous. She was a whole lot of women, and this had progressed way faster than I had expected. Well, not knowing how to make a move or knowing any better, I did nothing but talk. Kim just pranced around. Fuck, she was hot, and she constantly gave off sexual energy. We had another drink while skirting around what was about to happen when she just suddenly came out and said, "Why don't you go and take a shower, and I'll give you a blowjob."

I nearly fell of the couch! I said, "Are you for real? Did you just say that?" And believe it or not she was serious. "Show me the shower," I said, and shower I did. My cock was pumped up the whole shower is what I remember, and when I got out and dried off, I sat on her couch with a towel around me with my cock ready. Just like I'd been imagining Kim, she had been imagining the same thing all along as well. This was great, and I was going to enjoy this.

Kim came over got down on her knees in front of me. She opened the towel and proceeded to kiss, lick, and suck my cock and balls. It was spectacular! I was enjoying her work on my cock but was still a little anxious as I had only just met her. I couldn't believe where we were already. Here was this stunningly sexy woman, artfully sucking on my cock. I knew I would cum soon as she was really working it, and I was so turned on, when she just suddenly stopped. She got up and lifted her tiny skirt up, raised her leg over me, pulled her panties aside, and placed my cock at her pussy. She straddled me and climbed on. She really was horny, as she said. She eased me inside herself, and I watched the pleasure on her face as she started to ride me. She rode me slowly at first but then increasingly more vigorously. The more she rode me, the faster she got. She was full-on too. She really fucked me vigorously. I hadn't been fucked like that before. In fact, I'd never been fucked at all. This was something different. She held the back of my neck tightly with her tits pushing into my face, whipping her pelvis up and down on my shaft so fast, gyrating and angling herself for maximum pleasure until she made herself climax. It was quite spectacular to watch, and I didn't mind a bit. She just used me as a sexual implement and grinded my cock where she wanted it. I came just after she climaxed and pumped up into her hard, holding her waist tightly. It was a great fuck.

We both caught our breath and then she headed for a shower. *What a great fuck*, I thought, but now I wanted to head off. The thought of her boyfriend wouldn't leave my mind. Also, the fact that I was a dirty cheater was always playing a tune. She assured me he wouldn't come, and she kind of pleaded with me to stay, suggesting there was plenty more to come. I was only going to be at home that night, so I thought why not give her some more. She wasn't wrong, either. I joined her in the shower, and we gave each other a nice rub clean and then headed to her bedroom, where we dined on each other for a couple of hours. I gave her the best oral she had received in a long time, so she said. She wondered why I was so good at it. I had no idea I was, I told her. It just felt like the right thing for her. She was so hot. She liked it and really enjoyed my young strong body. She loved that I would fuck her rough too, as she put it, but it was more just in response to her aggressiveness in the sexual act. She was quite strong herself if still very feminine but liked going at it hard. She would really work and grind my cock and slam herself into me. I'd never experienced a woman who fucked quite like her. I left her house at around midnight and headed home. She made me promise that I would see her again soon. No demands, though—she just wanted the sex. She thought I was so handsome and hot and loved my hard cock. I couldn't believe my luck.

JOURNAL ENTRY FEBRUARY

Kim the Receptionist

Yesterday I fucked the receptionist from an engineering company where we clean the windows. Her name was Kim, and she would be in her forties. She was incredibly sexy, and we met up at a pub by the bay and had a couple of drinks after work. After this she invited me back to her place, and we had sex multiple times. She came onto me by telling me to "go and have a shower and I'll give you a blowjob." I'm still stunned. It was amazing, and I'm going back for more soon.

FROM THEN ON

Over the next year Kim was ready to have sex anywhere, anytime, at the beach, in her car, at her flat, or my house. She was always easy and up for some. She loved me licking her out. She loved it at night and one in the morning before work. She used to insist I just climb on and fuck her in the mornings before leaving for work, no foreplay, no asking—just fuck her and leave. She liked our relationship. It was just sex, and I could come and fuck her as often as I liked. She had an on-and-off relationship with her long-time boyfriend and was enjoying her freedom was how she used to put it. I fucked her for about a year until we had a big falling out. She had gotten jealous over me being with another woman one weekend, and she just went insane. I never really thought we had anything but sex, but apparently I was wrong. We lost the windows just after that. I can still see her today. It was a beautiful thing. It was a pity as she loved to fuck and let me anytime I wanted. I could have fixed it up with her, I thought, because she really loved our sex, but I was getting plenty elsewhere, so time to move on. Oh well, all good things come to an end. I wonder now at this time of writing whether she had another relationship going on as well? More than likely I think for someone who loved sex as much as Kim. I wasn't around enough to keep her happy, or was I? It would explain her psychotic break as well, maybe.

Kim and I had a crazy and at sometimes turbulent relationship. She had an ex-boyfriend when I first met her but was always ready to fuck me anytime we could get together. She would sometimes be quite insane about life, and she had this on-and-off relationship with her boyfriend. She loved fucking me but couldn't come to terms with the fact that I was so much younger, and we could never have a real relationship. She did, however, just love sex, so that's mostly what we did, and we only got in trouble when we strayed beyond this. If this doesn't make sense, then that's because I was quite often confused myself with this incredibly sexy and erotically beautiful woman.

VICTORIAN BITTER

LATE FEBRUARY 1985

In late February on a particularly hot day, a real stinker of about forty degrees, I was working alone as a few of the guys took holidays in the summer. I was on my last job for the day, and I remember being quite tired. I had been fucking Roni and was now being fucked relentlessly by Kim whenever I wanted. It was a great time; I was having so much sex. I never had a day or night off, and that was just how I liked it. I also had the girlfriend, who was none the wiser, as she only wanted it fortnightly, if that, or so it seemed. Thank fuck we didn't live together as this enabled me to get with Kim whenever I wanted. Literally the day before this Roni and I had one of our liaisons. Roni had mentioned we would have to stop this as it was going too far and that her husband would find out eventually. I think now she was really falling for me and was driven crazy by her fucked-up relationship and me and her.

Anyhow, a lot was going on, and I had decided not to go over to Roni's for a while, so I was working late. It was a Thursday arvo, and I was planning on going to football training, having a few beers, then calling on Kim. At least that's what I was thinking.

I headed to the last job on my sheet. It was a quote and in an apartment next to the beach just south of the city. When I arrived, an attractive woman, probably late twenties, greeted me wearing just a T-shirt over a bright-coloured bikini, and I remember thinking, *Wow! You got my attention.* I acted professional, however, and started the job. It was a hot late afternoon, and I was wearing only shorts and a singlet. I had literally been dripping in sweat all afternoon, and it was nice and cool in her apartment. She had just moved in, and the agent had arranged for the internal windows to be done. She was very excited to be having them cleaned—or so it seemed at first, but then she informed me that she had just broken up with her boyfriend and had moved out. It was an emotional time, and she was getting used to the adjustment.

I felt like a counsellor listening to people's problems sometimes. It was part of the job. I didn't mind so much as she was tight to look at, but I was mostly thinking about getting done and heading home. She then offered me a beer, a Victorian Bitter. This is a popular beer in my town, and I would usually have said no because drinking in the arvo wasn't something I usually did, but it was so hot, I just thought, *Oh, what the fuck, why not.* She pulled a cold stubby out of the fridge and gave it to me, then said to make myself at home and that she was going to go for a swim and to yell out when I was done. I thanked her and said I would get into the job. Her apartment was on the third level, and from her balcony I could see down to the communal pool courtyard. I was only cleaning the insides and balcony windows, so the job was only going to take me about 20 minutes. Because of this and the fact that she had left me, I decided to take a seat and enjoy the beer.

As soon as the beer hit my lips, I remember feeling fantastic. It was one of the greatest beers of my life: so cold, so refreshing, so stimulating. I sucked it down so fast and enjoyed it so much that I really wanted another one. It was just what I needed after how hard I'd been working day and night, ha ha. I wanted to just go to her fridge and grab another but was not about to do that, so I got stuck into the windows. I started on the kitchen, and it was then I noticed her down by the pool. She was pretty tight, great body, slim, cute little tits, and sweet-looking arse, and she looked very fuckable lying on the deck chair. She had this bright fluoro pink-and-green bikini that stood out like neon. When I came out onto her balcony to do the window, I had another look at her. She saw me and asked if everything was okay. I was a bit embarrassed, as she had caught me out having a perv. I thought she must have known it. I just shouted back, "All good, thanks."

With that I stopped fucking around and got into the job. I really felt like another beer, though, and had decided to ask her for another when the job was finished, even if I had to pay for it. Anyhow, I was doing the last windows in her bedroom when she arrived back. I thought, *Oh, fuck she's suss on me for perving at her, it's made her come back up. Oh well,* I thought just as quickly. *I can ask her for another beer now.* She came into the bedroom and asked, "How's it going?"

"No problems," I said, thanking her for the beer and saying how nice it was for her to give me one and that I had enjoyed it so much, could I possibly get another one? Also, I was happy to pay. It was just that it was so hot, and it had gone down so well and fast.

She laughed and said, "No worries! I wondered why you were looking down at me." She was only wearing her bikini now, which was grouse! I was getting a nice eyeful. She went to get another, and I finished the window in the bedroom. When I turned around, she was standing there holding an open stubby in just her bikini, legs crossed at the front, shoulders back, really showing herself off, I thought. She handed it toward me, but I was just stunned. I said, "Wow, I like your bikini." Her sweet, gorgeous body was tanned all over, and she had long golden hair that flowed forever down her back. I was starting to blush.

She thanked me and said it was nice to have some company and that she had been lonely since her breakup, looking at me pitifully. I took a monster scull of the beer, and that was it; we were into it. Her bikini top was off as soon as I grabbed her. I sucked on her little titties hard, smothering them with my mouth. She gave into me completely. I sucked on her neck, we kissed passionately, and I mouthed her everywhere, all the time groping her tight little arse, with my fingers quickly finding her wet hole. I fingered her vigorously, first with one finger, then two and then three, really giving her a good go. I pushed her back onto the bed and began sucking on her pussy and arsehole for what felt like an hour. She was delightful. I fucked her with my tongue as deep as it would go into her arse. She loved it. She howled. At times I came up for a breather and she jerked my cock hard and sucked on it furiously whenever she got the chance. I was in heaven. Her arse was just so tight and spread so delightfully that I was constantly wanting to suck on it some more, like a juicy ripe orange, and I slobbered away. Eventually when I had finally had enough, I fucked her doggie style so fast and hard the mattress came off the base. At the end I pulled out and turned her around, quickly putting it in her mouth. She didn't hesitate and tried sucking it all down, but she choked and half of it went over her face. It was just totally uninhibited sex at its best, no holding back. We both fell on the mattress completely spent, panting away. When I got my breath, I got up and grabbed the stubby I had left it on the windowsill before we went at it. I gulped the rest down. I put on my shorts, and she grabbed me another beer and put her bikini on, and we both headed down for a swim. We copped a few weird looks from neighbours who had obviously heard the commotion. Oh well, it was just window cleaning. I swam and hung out with her for about half an hour and then found out her name was Michelle. She gave me her number and invited me over again if I wanted. I said I would call and then left. A great fuck! I loved sucking on her. Some women just make me want to do that more. I was really starting to notice a trend. It was hard to stop thinking about what had just happened while driving back. I was buzzing from the booze and the incredible surprise sex I had just had. I loved a surprise hot fuck with a stranger, topped off with a nice cool swim. It was so hot my shorts dried quickly, and I remember getting to football training and wanting to share this with someone, but I didn't. I just ran around and trained hard. I put down my thoughts in my journal later that night and slept very well.

FROM THE JOURNAL

Today I had the most splendid surprise fuck with another client while on the job. This seems to be becoming a bit of a habit, and I'm looking forward to it continuing. Her name was Michelle, and we fucked in her bedroom after she had given me a couple of beers. She was very attractive, slim, and a great fuck. She came into the bedroom while I was cleaning the window wearing just her bikini. After giving me the second beer, we just went at it. She had just broken up with her boyfriend, so I think this helped me get this fuck. I was an emotional rebound bit of sex. I love being used in this way.

FROM THEN ON

I really liked Michelle. We had made a real connection and became friends—sort of. We talked a lot and always seemed to be trying to give each other helpful life advice. If I wasn't with my girlfriend, I probably could have had a relationship with her. She would have made a great girlfriend. Probably I would have cheated on her anyway, as all I did was fuck around any chance I got. It would never have worked, and she knew this. It was for the best when she left town, and I'm sure she would have found her way.

TWISTING BY THE POOL

LATE FEBRUARY 1985

After the game on Saturday my girlfriend, Angela, was heading out with her friends on a girls' night, so I decided to give Michelle a call. I hadn't been able to get her out of my head. The sex was so passionate and uninhibited I wanted a repeat. Thoughts of those sweet little titties and gorgeous arse were hard to get out of my head. I could taste her just thinking about her. We spoke on the phone briefly. I felt a bit awkward, and she invited me around the next day for a swim, she called it. It was going to be another scorcher so it sounded good to me. I couldn't wait. Anyhow, I'd been hoping to see her that night, so instead I headed to the club to get on the drink with the boys, then it was out on the prowl. After a big night of drinking and bombing out, I was off to Kim's house, knocking on her door around two o'clock in the morning. Inside I went, and we fucked for a couple of hours, falling asleep around 4:00 a.m. I was wreaked.

The next day I didn't stir till about nine, when I woke to Kim sucking and jerking my cock. Well, there was no sleeping now, so I let it happen. I was getting close when she decided to straddle me. She rode up and down hard, as usual getting herself off! She always did that. I didn't mind. I found it quite a turn on. She would get so into it you could do anything to her. I'd squeezed her tits hard, pull her hair, bite her. She loved it. Once she climaxed on top of me, I flipped her over and fucked her doggie. It didn't take me long until I squirted deep inside her, slamming her arse hard and fast and then holding on for a tight connection at the end for a deep finish. I loved it also. After recovering and a shower, she made me breakfast. We chatted and chilled for a while, and I left around midday, telling her I was heading home to rest.

Really, I was going to catch up with my girlfriend, as I hadn't seen her since early yesterday evening. I gave her a call when I got home, and she was crook. The girls had had a big night on the drink, and she wasn't going anywhere or doing anything. She did want me to come around, though, as she needed a cuddle. She wanted to just laze in and get a video, so I went over. Angela lived with three other older girls: Karen, Prue, and Nicole. The latter two were nurses. They were all wrecked from the night before. They were watching some chick-flick shit that was boring. As I'd come in late, I didn't know what it was about. I chilled on the couch for a while and when it ended, I decided to leave.

I never really enjoyed all the girls in her household. They were a bit stuck up and thought they were better than my girlfriend and me—well, at least me, I thought. Nowadays I think I felt nervous around them because I knew how unfaithful I was. I was a dirty rotten cheater. It was about 4:00 p.m. and stinking hot. I was thinking about that swim with Michelle. Angela didn't want me to go, but I told her I was tired too from the weekend and wanted an early night. She begged me to stay, but I just wasn't feeling it. Really, I wanted to call on Michelle and get my end in. I did hang around for another hour, then headed off and got home by about 6:00 p.m.

I was now tired and feeling awkward about not going to Michelle's, especially after I said I would, so I decided to call and apologise. I was just going to make up some bullshit excuse. I was getting so much sex from Kim at this point and with Roni and occasionally Angela, I could afford a night off. When she answered, I could tell she was a bit tipsy, and I could also hear some cheering in the background. I apologised for not making it, but she was still eager for me to come around. There was still plenty of daylight left, and it was still stinking hot, so I said, "Why not? If you're that keen also."

The sound of her voice made my cock stir, so I headed over. I was excited. I was going to have sex with this little hottie again. It was about a half an hour drive from my place, and when I arrived, I thought, *Shit, I should have brought some beer at least to replace for the other day.* Oh well, it was getting late, so I just headed in. As I knocked on her door, I was excited and then got a big surprise when a different woman opened the door. There was a cheer and a whoop. Shit, she had friends over. I was suddenly out of my comfort zone as I was expecting us to be alone and go at it again.

Damn women—they can be very unpredictable, I thought. Michelle skipped over. She'd definitely been drinking and introduced me to Kasey and Belinda. They all looked like they had been drinking for a while. They had a go at me for taking so long to come around and said they had heard all about my window cleaning services and laughed hysterically. I felt a bit awkward at first but then started to relax as I could see they were impressed. Kasey was overtly checking me out, and Michelle gave me a beer. We chatted for a bit before heading down to the pool. As we walked down, I started to think, *How crazy is this? I would fuck all these girls any day.* Kasey and Belinda were very tidy indeed. Kasey was a tall, slim, pale brunette with a crooked little smile. She had tiny titties like Michelle. Belinda, well, she was just as cute as a button. She had bottle-blonde hair and was shorter than the others but had a beautiful body with big full breasts and a nice chunky butt. She also had tattoos, something I hadn't really seen on a woman before. It made her even sexier. They looked great, I thought. One of them ran across the front of her bikini line, making you want to look there constantly, and I wondered how far it went. We swam in the pool playfully together. They were all well primed, with Michelle running back up to her apartment to get me refills when I finished.

When Michelle went up to get me my first refill, Kasey jumped on me in the pool, wrestling playfully. I got a hold of her and felt her up good. Her arse felt delightful, and she just boldly squeezed my cock. I was stiffening fast, and I just let her go for it. She had a good long feel and squeezed me nicely, gave it a bit of a stroke through my shorts. I was going to fuck this one. I didn't know when, where, or how, but it was going to happen. I had a few more beers, and we all lazed around as the sun went down. It was still stinking hot. At this point Michelle suggested we take this party upstairs and cool off with the air-conditioning. I sensed something going on but was in no way expecting what was about to happen.

We headed off to the apartment. As we started to head up, I stopped to take a piss in the poolside communal toilet. I was quite relaxed by now and wondering where this night would take me. Suddenly the door crashed open with all the girls giggling and wanting to see my cock and watch me pissing. They were laughing, quite drunk, and saying, "Let's have a look at it. We've heard so much about it." I was pissing a fountain having drunk three stubbies, and both Kasey and Belinda groped away. This was crazy. What was I, a sex toy? I didn't know if Michelle realised what a horny slut Kasey was but now Belinda as well. She shook my cock when I finished pissing and started to jerk me off, saying, "We've heard everything about you."

Kasey then started sucking my cock as soon as I finished pissing. She didn't even care that she was getting some of my piss. Belinda pulled my cock away from her and wacked her in the face with it and continued to jerk away. The two of them played, giggling and laughing loudly. I just stood there and enjoyed the action. At first I thought it was just a bit of a drunken game, but these two wanted some cock. While they continued to play, I started groping Belinda's arse and tits. Suddenly Michelle crashed in and demanded that we go up to the apartment or she would probably lose her lease. I packed myself away as much as I could because I was now at nearly full mast, and we all headed upstairs.

When the door on the apartment shut, the action began. Kasey and Belinda just stripped me naked, pulling down my shorts. They both went for my cock. This was incredible. Michelle came over, and we pashed she caressed my body. These three hotties were just all over me. I started to wonder how I was going to go here, but then just got lost in it all. I started grabbing and kissing and tonguing and licking. I fucked Kasey first doggie, as she just asked for it, and it was then that I noticed the other two chewing on each other. Wow, this was cool. I fucked Kasey hard and fast as I was really revving up. It was very exciting. After pumping her doggie style for a good time, I got off her and then jumped into Michelle, as her sweet arse was high in the air while she pleasured Belinda. I gave her a good go while looking down at Belinda, who was stuffing Michelle's face into her snatch. I was ready to cum when Kasey grabbed me and started to suck me. I lost my load at that point, and the other girls gathered around. They licked it up, kissing each other and then just continuing to roll around together, never mind me.

This was amazing. I remember hearing the song "Twisting by the Pool" by Dire Straits, which seemed to capture the beat of the encounter. My orgasm didn't stop the girls. They were all over each other, and I was soon as well. I licked and sucked on boobs, pussy, and arse, whatever I liked. Once I'd hardened up fully again, I fucked them all, making sure they all were happy and that I gave them all a good go. It was the greatest, and it seemed like I could fuck forever. I came the second time, pulling out onto Belinda's chunky butt. Kasey was there smacking and squeezing my arse as I roared in climax. That was a first for me, as was it all. I lay back and watched the three of them continue. They were very good friends. I thought to myself, *Where am I?*

They coaxed me back in one more time. It didn't take much really. Looking at those three sweet arses got me stirring, and once I started eating pussy, I was soon stiff and hard again. I spent time licking both Kasey and Belinda out, making them both climax multiple times. It was what they really wanted. They, like all my new encounters, just loved having their pussies licked. Roni was right, I thought. They all then got another go of the shaft in so many different positions that I can hardly remember who I did in which way, but it was great, and we eventually finished. I was so exhausted and so it, seemed, were they. My cock had been sucked and jerked so much by these three, and I'd fucked them all multiple times. I was really feeling like a stud, and my cock needed a break. I don't know what time it was, but we all crashed out in the one bed, all tangled together. When I woke at first light, the bed was a mess of naked bodies. I got up and took a piss. I couldn't believe what had happened, and I was wrecked. I also had to head off to work. Standing there naked, looking at these three naked hotties, I just smiled. I got dressed after finding my shorts, grabbed my thongs and shirt, and went back to say goodbye. The three of them were dead asleep, so I just left.

I DO LIKE MONDAYS

That day at work I felt like a God. I remember it well. I told Bob what had happened, and he was gobsmacked. "You're a lucky bastard," he kept saying and suggesting I introduce him. You could smell the women on me all day. When I went to the toilet and pulled out my cock, all I could smell was sex. We laughed and talked about women all day. It was a very good day. When we finished around 1:00 p.m., I headed home. I was so physically tired and needed a rest. The thought did go through my head to drop by Michelle's and say hello, but I was wrecked, and I'd had more sex in twenty-four hours than I thought anyone needed, so I headed home for a rest. I had been with four women in twenty-four hours, and we're talking multiple times. When I got home, I wrote about the encounter in the journal. I also spent some time writing about Roni and Kim. I was amazed by what was happening to me. For years I had been very awkward with women, wanting to have sex and be confident with them but never really able to make it happen. My sexual encounters prior to these were just one-night stands and with Angela. I mean, I enjoyed them, but all I had ever done was just intercourse, never any real oral, and I had certainly never delivered any. I'd considered it disgusting. I never considered going down on a one-night stand. It just never happened, and with Angela it never happened either. I didn't want it to. There was just something amiss with us, and I couldn't figure it out.

With these new women, however, oral sex was the go. Roni had got me started and really educated me by letting me do her so often. She talked about sex so openly with me in a way I had never experienced. I mean, the only time I had talked about sex prior was with my mates, and I can tell you most blokes have no idea. Roni told me how she needed oral to climax and that it had to be part of it for her and all women. She could climax during intercourse, but it was usually after being pleasured orally. She enjoyed it so much that I found it a massive turn on. Roni's moans and cries of delight hardened me so much that it intensified our sexual encounters or, as I had started to think about it, our lovemaking. It was a real sexual education, the type I had never had access to before, and I was an eager and fast-learning student.

Kim was just a nymphomaniac. She called herself an insomniac nympho, and as mentioned she was like sex on a stick. When you looked at her, you just thought sex. I was always happy to go down on her for the same reasons I did with Roni. It just made for the most intense sex I had ever had or could imagine. I would chew on her for ages.

Now with Michelle I could just eat her pussy and arse all day long. I don't know what it was exactly. Well, they were all spectacular women with the tightest arses and sweetest vaginas, but I was becoming an oral monster, and the ladies loved it. I had even heard Kasey say, "We've heard you're a giver," and I was finally realising this was making me more desirable to women and more sexually confident. I knew how to get a woman to orgasm, something I had no idea about in the past, and I could do it more than once. I was in control. They wanted me more and more, and I was making them fantasize about me like I was fantasizing about them. Interesting! I was more confident with these newfound powers I thought. Perhaps I could be some kind of superhero: Dickman. Dickman to the rescue, rescuing damsels in distress of not having great sex. How about the evil and mysterious pussy muncher? I knew Kim liked a bad boy and even told me how she fantasised about being raped. We tried playing it out one time with me breaking into her bedroom window. It went well. I fucked her with a balaclava on, and she loved it.

Anyway, with my journal now up to date, I relaxed and just thought about how I was going to negotiate all these women and not let Angela find out. I was playing it well, I thought. So far none of the girls had my phone number or knew where I lived. They also didn't know about each other. Roni was talking about stopping because of her husband. Kim was sex whenever

I liked without obligation, and Michelle and her band—
well, who knew? I would just call on them when I felt
like it and see what happened. Angela would be none
the wiser. What a guy! Also, there would be whatever
other encounters I could make happen. Life seemed
very good. I was getting plenty of sex, and as far as I
was concerned that was all that life was about. That's
really what I thought at this point in my life. Tonight,
however, I was staying home as somebody needed a rest.
My cock was sore. I remember thinking it hadn't felt
like this since I was a young fella, still a teenager. When
I first discovered masturbation, I had pulled it so often
back then that I had worn some skin off and made it
bleed. Probably too much information, but since were
sharing… It was nasty.

I called Angela and spoke for an hour. She begged
me to come over as she was in the mood. I got out
of it, though, and promised her Tuesday we'd do it.
I then called Michelle from the pay phone down the
road. I wanted to talk to her about what had happened,
especially since I'd left before they were awake. She was
cool, and we talked for about half an hour. She asked
for my number, and I told her I was calling from a pay
phone. She said, "You've got a girlfriend, don't you?"

I said no, but it didn't fool her. I was a hopeless liar.
I said the phone was not connected because I'd just
moved to a new house with some people. I told her
that once it was on, I'd give it to her. I asked her if she
wanted to catch up again, and she wasn't sure. She told
me Kasey really wanted my number. "Are you okay
with that?" I asked.

She just laughed and said, "No one can stop Kasey. Pussy or cock—if she wants it, she gets it."

I told her I'd call her later in the week and that I would love another swim. Michelle said, "Okay, why not?" Fuck! I needed some sleep.

I stayed at Angela's house the next night, and true to her word she was in the mood for some loving. We did it the usual way, nothing too exciting. We pashed for a bit, a bit of a grope and then I was in her missionary style. That was the usual. Sometimes we might go doggie, but it always seemed like it was an effort for Angela or even painful. I did give it to her a bit harder than usual as I was thinking about all the other girls, and I just decided to fuck her hard. For some reason sex for us was a struggle. It just didn't seem as magical as it should be. Neither of us would confront it, though, and now that I was getting my dick sucked all over town, I didn't have any attention on it at all. My attention now was on only how I could continue to have all the uninhibited sex I could get without Angela finding out about it. I was in love with her, and I knew this would devastate her, so it was best to keep it a secret. That was how I thought back then. I really didn't have any idea at all about what it took to have a great relationship. I just thought everyone rooted around and that it was normal, but whatever you do, don't get caught.

The next day I called Michelle. I was worried that she thought I had a girlfriend and that I wouldn't give her my number, so I decided to give it to her. The chances of Angela ever answering a call at my place were slim, or so I thought, and I was kind of interested in catching up with Kasey soon, especially if she was interested in me. I called Michelle after I finished work, around two. She was home alone and was happy for me to come over. I was really in the mood. Just the thought of this girl and her friends drove me crazy. I just couldn't get the thoughts of them out of my head. I was a man on a mission.

When I arrived, I thought to myself again, *No beer*, so I got back in my car and drove to the nearest bottle shop. I returned with a six-pack of Vic Bitter and a little gift teddy bear that they had on sale. I thought, *What the hell? She might like it.* I knew girls liked stuff like that.

Well, I was right. She loved it. She started crying when I gave her the teddy and just hugged me. I sat her down and held her for a while. She was emotional and upset. We spoke and she was really doing hard after her breakup. She was still in love with her ex, but he was very unfaithful, and she just couldn't take it. She said her behaviour this last week was unusual and not really her.

I felt for her. It was sad to see her so unhappy. I really felt like helping, but there wasn't much I could do. I was just really interested in fucking her and her friends, but I would help if I could and if that meant just having a chin wag today instead of fucking, then so be it. I was also pretty sure I could get with Kasey or Belinda, and there was always my ever-reliable Kim waiting in the wings. I hadn't fucked her since Sunday. She'd be aching for some, I thought. What a guy I was! I suggested to Michelle that we have a drink and just talk—maybe we could work something out. I didn't have any idea really, but it felt like the right thing to do, so we did. I cracked a couple of beers, and we sat back on her couch talking. I owned up about having a girlfriend and the challenges we had in our relationship. She then started giving me advice and telling me what a scumbag I was for rooting around. She was right, of course, but I couldn't change what had happened and could only work toward the future. I suggested the same for her.

Michelle was older and I guess closer to wanting to settle down and marry. I told her that if this guy didn't shape up, there would be plenty more eligible guys out there for a beautiful woman like her. She was flattered, and it cheered her up. It was true too; if this guy didn't want her, I thought what a loser. I cracked another beer by now and another for Michelle. I thought it was going well. I was a real solutions guy as she had cheered up. We talked about the foursome, and she told me that she had never done anything like that before. "No kidding, me either," I said. "It was incredible."

"Kasey and Belinda are bisexual. Once I told them about my window cleaner, they were desperate to meet you and add you to their collection. They had been waiting for hours and you were never going to leave the other night without giving up some cock. They enjoyed you too. Kasey really wants to get with you again."

I asked about Belinda because I really liked her too, but Michelle warned me not to go there. "Belinda has a biker for a boyfriend, and he would cut your balls off if he found out you fucked her. He doesn't mind that she's bisexual because he gets to fuck her friends, but he won't like you, and he's one guy I'd stay away from, a real dirt bag."

Fair enough, I thought. I don't need any headaches. Michelle said, "You can have Kasey's number, though. I said I would give it to you." She got up and wrote it down on a piece of paper. I put it in my wallet.

I felt a bit bad, but I was also excited thinking about getting with Kasey. I asked her if she was okay, and she nodded. The talk and beer had lightened her up and I sensed an opening. It wasn't premeditated. I would have been happy to go at that point, but I was also happy to stay. I rubbed her leg gently and she sank into me. We started to kiss and then continued further, making love slowly on the couch. I kissed her gently all over her neck and face. It felt like what she needed. I took my time for a change. There was no rush. We got more heated as we went on undressing each other. I was dirty from working, but it didn't bother Michelle. She sucked my cock beautifully. I nearly came and pushed her off so I could have a go at her. I loved her arse. I would miss this, I thought, but maybe it was the last time. I spent a while licking, sucking, kissing, and chewing her pussy. I loved making a slobbering mess as she climaxed several times. I also used my tongue like a cock, jabbing it in and out of her. I also spent a good amount of time licking and sticking my tongue in her arsehole. She loved that. I did too. In the end I fucked her doggie quite vigorously while inserting my thumb up her arse. She squealed in climax at this, and it seemed right. I came deep inside her, thrusting hard with every pump while she wailed, holding inside at the end, catching our breaths until my cock eventually softened and slid out. It was awkward after that, so I left saying I'd call her later to see how things were. I headed home.

FROM THEN ON

I continued to fuck Michelle on a weekly basis for about two months. After that she had had enough and moved to Sydney. She wanted a fresh start and had been offered some work up there. She asked me if I wanted to come. It shocked me at first. I was like, "How can I?" She knew I had a girlfriend. Just goes to show what a dickhead and how self-absorbed I was. Michelle had really fallen for me, and all the time I was just rooting around, taking no responsibility and treating her as a sex toy once a week. She deserved better, so she left. I never heard from her again.

HAWAIIAN FLING

Estelle, Advertising Executive
March 1985

I was working with Simon this day. After we had finished our shop run, we got some breakfast. The word had gotten out about my foursome, and he wanted all the grit. I filled him in while we did the shops and as we ate. He loved it. Turned out he had a few tales of his own, and he was still rooting one woman he'd met at a job on a semiregular basis. He also told me a few stories of some of the other guys at the company. It seemed that everyone had just about had some kind of experience, and there would be more to come. He said, "It's inevitable a lot of these women are crying out for it, mate." I agreed. It seemed to me that every day now, some woman somewhere on some job would flirt or check me out or give me the eye. Whatever you want to call it, there was always a woman somewhere who wanted it. It wasn't just me, it seemed. All these girls, ladies, women, wanted sex, and if we could oblige then so be it. Lots of women were not satisfied sexually, and this opened the door for us, I thought. Simon agreed and shared that there was also the fantasy aspect to this. He told me that a lot of women have it as a fantasy to fuck the window cleaner or be fucked by him, he told me as he clutched his cock. Simon was a man's man—a real tough and wild bastard. He had really long red hair was about six feet tall with broad shoulders and tattoos. You wouldn't stuff around with him, that's for sure. Simon was the toughest at the company bar none. I could tell he had an edge of lunacy. You wouldn't want to get on his wrong side.

After breakfast we were meeting a couple of the other crews at an advertising firm close to the city. It was a big job, and the boys had already started when we arrived. Simon said, "C'mon, let's get in there. There's bound to be some nice pussy in there."

I laughed and thought he was probably right. The last thing I needed now was any more pussy. I was so busy now I couldn't even imagine another woman, much less how I'd fit her into my schedule as I was fully booked. My last week had been like this:

Monday: Kasey

Tuesday: Kasey

Wednesday: Roni and Angela

Thursday: Kim

Friday: Angela

Saturday: Angela

Sunday: Kim and Michelle (not together but one after the other)

It was crazy. That is a full book by anyone's estimation, and it was tricky trying to keep it all quiet around Angela. I did have sex with Angela only once that week, but she still demanded a time commitment of at least two nights a week, and lately it seemed like she wanted to increase that. She didn't want any more sex, just wanted me around. She was in love and missed me terribly when I didn't stay. She liked to cuddle up and just be a couple. The more I was with her, the harder it was to keep up with my other girls. They needed sex, and I loved delivering it. The idea of adding another at this stage was crazy.

Anyhow, back to the advertising agency job. Simon and I headed inside only to be shooed out by the other crews. They had the inside under control and wanted us to start on the outside. Shane said, "Fuck that! I'm doing inside."

No one argued with him. So I just headed out and got started in this courtyard. It was a two-story building, so I needed a ladder. I got into it, enjoying the sun, and was basically off in my own world, minding my own business, going up and down the ladder from one window to the next. It's kind of a relaxing job really, once you're good at it. You can basically do it with your eyes shut. It doesn't take much thinking. As I got up to one window, it was open. I started to pull it closed to clean it and heard a voice say abruptly, "Don't close that!"

It startled me, as I was in my own world. Also there was something striking about the voice. I said, "I'll need to shut it if I'm going to clean it." I still hadn't laid eyes on the person with the voice, then suddenly I was staring at this gorgeous Sheila—or at least her tits. Wow, she was stunning. She was abrupt and told me to please hurry and she liked the fresh air. There was something funny about her accent. "Okay," I whispered. "Have a whinge, why don't you." I cleaned her window, taking my time to wipe the ledge and perving in to have another look at her. She was fucking spectacular, or at least that's what it looked like from on top of a ladder through old glass. It was hard to tell fully, but she seemed to have all the right bits. I raised the window back up and yelled out, "All done." She just put up her hand and scowled at me. I then noticed she was on the phone, so I went away. Shit, this was the sort of thing that customers complained about, I thought, so I continued as quickly and quietly as I could after that.

Simon and the others came out and started outside as well. They were done inside, and all of them were yapping about the women inside: "She's stacked," and "What an arse," and "Did you see those legs? I'd love to get between them." I just smiled. The boys got going on the outside of the building, and I continued around the courtyard. I was on the last window up the ladder when I noticed the lady I'd disturbed was watching me. I acted as if I didn't know at first, then I thought, *She's having a perv—another one that wants a go.* I got off the ladder turned and looked up at her. She was smiling now, not scowling. That was good. She's been checking me out, I could tell. Enjoying my arse. These tight football shorts didn't leave much to the imagination, and she'd been having a good look. I smiled back and nodded, packing the ladder up in one smooth move, throwing it up onto my shoulder like a he-man and marching it out to the wagon. I was like a strutting rooster, showing her how strong I was.

I returned to start on the lower windows in the courtyard only to be greeted by this stunning woman. She said hello and complimented me on my work. "You're doing a super job." She had a strong American accent. I thanked her and went about cleaning the ground-floor windows. I found her beauty quite intimidating for some reason and felt nervous. I mean, just a little while ago she had screamed at me to get away as I was bothering her. Now she was having a cigarette and asked me if I would like one.

I told her, "No, I don't smoke, but thanks anyway."

She was stunning and tall, probably about five foot eleven, long brown hair, beautiful eyes, and a smile that just drew you in. She was very slender with big tits and an amazing-looking arse at the top of those legs. I could hardly believe what she was wearing. She had the tiniest denim miniskirt that just barely covered her arse. Her legs literally went forever. The belt on the miniskirt was almost as big as the skirt, and on top she had a blue-and-white hooped T-shirt thing that plunged at the front, showing off the most spectacular set of tits. Oh, and of course she had heels on. I was completely flustered at this point because she was smoking hot. I could feel that she was interested in me, and for some reason I couldn't relax. I think it was because I was working, and I thought the other guys would come around any minute. I don't really know.

I managed to ask her where she was from, and I told her I loved her accent. She smiled and said, "I don't have an accent."

"To me, you do," I said. She also loved our Aussie accents. We both laughed. Turned out she was from Hawaii and was out on assignment for her advertising company. I asked her how she was enjoying Australia, and she just lit up. She was loving it. The whole time while we were talking, she was sucking on the cigarette. She kept flicking her hair and stretching her body, really putting on a bit of a show—not that she needed to. She sat for a minute, and I couldn't help but see her undies. Those legs and short skirt just drew my eyes in. She had to have noticed. We both looked at each other quietly for a moment and then she jumped up, saying she better let me get back to it. As she strode away, I couldn't help myself and said out loud, "You are beautiful." My jaw was probably open.

She turned and smiled. She was stunning! Perhaps I could fit another girl in my schedule, I thought. In fact, for her I would clear my whole calendar. She was too classy for me, though, I thought. I was a window cleaner, and she was like Miss Universe. I was a mess. I finished off the windows in the courtyard. As I walked out I noticed her looking at me and smiling from the window. I waved and smiled. I was gobsmacked; she was flirting with me. I didn't know what I could do at that point as we would be finishing soon, and I checked on where the other guys were up to. They were on the ground windows now, and Shane told me to take the ladders back to the vehicles. I grabbed the nearest one and returned it to our vehicle. I threw it on the roof rack and secured it. I turned to get the next one, when there she was, heading straight toward me. Fuck, she was hot. The way she strode toward me, tits bouncing, all legs and arse struggling to stay in that denim mini. I was in love, or lust, or both.

She held out her hand and introduced herself. "I'm Estelle!"

I shook her small soft hand and said, "I'm Dick."

I must have had the dumbest look on my face as she started laughing. "I'd really like to go out with you if you're interested after work for a drink and perhaps you could show me around? I don't really no anyone except the workers here, and anyway, here's my number if you're interested."

With that she spun around and strode off. She seemed embarrassed. I mumbled out, "Yeah, sure I'll give you a call. When's good?"

She turned back as sexy as fuck and said, "Anytime," then smiled and winked at me. I just stood there stunned, watching her wiggle her way back to her building. She looked back at me a couple of times before going inside. Wow! Fuck, what a dish! I could have jumped for joy at that moment. I was so excited. It was amazing. I found the flirting, the chase, the tease, the build-up, and all the lead-up stuff just so exciting. I was stoked. We packed up and left the job. When we got back to the office, the boys mentioned Estelle to the boss. No one knew her name but me, though, and I was about to find out a whole lot more.

When I got home, I was in a funk. I wanted to call her straight away, but I wanted to play it cool as well. I was such a dickhead. I mean, she came to me. I knew she was keen. Fuck, the way she was dressed and all and asking me out. It was a Wednesday night. Angela would be expecting me to come over. I gave her a call and told her I wasn't feeling well, and I'd be staying home. By seven o'clock I couldn't take it any longer. I gave Estelle a call. She answered with that beautiful accent, and I nervously mumbled out, "Hello, it's Dick, the window cleaner." She laughed but her voice softened, and we talked for about half an hour. She was so sexy on the phone; I couldn't help squeezing my cock from time to time. I could have just jerked off at the thought of her and her voice. Listening to her had made me quite horny. Still feeling awkward, I finally asked if she'd like to catch up tonight.

She said, "Sure. There is a bar downstairs from my apartment if you want to meet there."

"Sounds great. I will be there in about an hour." I quickly showered and headed over. I arrived at the bar around 8:30 p.m., having driven like a maniac.

When I arrived at the bar, I could see through the windows there was hardly anyone there, but I saw Estelle straight away before I even got inside. She was standing at the bar as I came in, and I could see that the barman was enjoying the view. You couldn't blame him, as she was out-of-this-world beautiful. She was eye-popping enough you could have put a bag over her head and fallen in love. She was wearing a white long-sleeve top that went to just below her spectacular boobs.

To top it off, though, it was see-through, and you could see the bright green bra she was wearing underneath. Her midriff was showing, and she had the tightest stretch jeans I've ever seen and of course a big belt. She saw me come in and greeted me with a kiss and then led me to a table. We shared a bottle of Champagne and just talked for an hour, laughing at each other's accents, with me basically schooling her on Australia. Beneath all the chat, though, was something else obvious to her and me, I'm sure. I was tingling from the champas and her company, as I'm sure she was as well.

She suggested we go for a walk. It was a good idea because I didn't really know how I was going to move things along from here, so we got up and went outside. As we walked, I got to really have a good look at her. She didn't mind either. I told her how beautiful she was, and she loved it, twirling around. She was so alive and happy to be out and about and said she had been a bit unsure to walk around at night in an unknown city. We walked the block, and on returning she invited me up to her apartment. This was exactly the in I was hoping for.

In the elevator we kissed passionately. She sank into me like we were two pieces in a puzzle. We were interrupted as the lift stopped and some others got inside. We laughed, holding each other until we reached her level. She had a beautiful apartment with a great view of the city to the north, but by far the best view was Estelle. We fell onto her couch, kissing passionately again. She was so spectacular. I kept stopping to admire her beauty, kissing her neck, ears, lips, biting and sucking. She was writhing like a goddess. In no time at all I had ripped off her top and removed her bra strap with one flick. I had become the master at that. I started on her breasts, again kissing and sucking passionately, trying not to go too fast but all the time being lost in this most erotic of encounters. I fondled and mouthed her tits for a long time. She moaned so pleasurably the whole time. We grinded against each other, pressing our groins together. My cock was bursting uncomfortably as usual in my jeans, so I stood up and released it. It sprang out so hard that it wacked Estelle in the chin, which was just the signal to get her to work.

She was so happy to see my cock. It was like she was a junkie that needed a fix. She admired it for a moment, telling me this was going to be good, then she sucked kissed and caressed me so well that I was unable to control myself and blew my load quite quickly. She swallowed it down—most of it anyway. I came so much it was dribbling down her chin. She wiped it away as I fell back on her couch. I still hadn't gotten my jeans off. *Oh no, what a fuck up,* I thought. I'd come to soon. I started to apologise, and she laughed and said, "Don't worry. I loved doing that."

I grabbed her, threw her over, and started kissing the back of her neck. She moaned nicely, and I continued down her back, kissing and caressing every inch, taking my time. It was her turn now, I decided, and I was going to give her the works. I was completely lost in her beauty. She arched her back as I got further down. I knew what she wanted and couldn't wait to get at her. She was not ready for what was coming, I was sure. When I got to her arse, I started to nibble her through her jeans. I spent quite some time kissing and nibbling through her jeans, my hands all the time rubbing her crotch. She continued to moan with pleasure. Eventually I buried my face right between her cheeks, pushing in hard with my mouth and really slobbering up the fabric of her jeans. I could smell and taste her through the fabric.

She had had enough at some point, demanding I take them off. I came up for air as she undid the front of her jeans, her head giving her balance while she quickly undid the buttons. I gave her arse a wack, which she liked. She was so turned on I was going to be able to do anything. I tugged her jeans down around her, splayed out her arse. They were tight, so it took a bit of effort, I jerked at them hard and wiggled her from side to side. I could see she didn't mind being thrown around. Her arse was spectacular and with her jeans so tight she was restricted in her movement like she was tied around the thighs. I kissed the naked flesh of her arse cheeks, which I licked with excitement. She was arching her back so much I could tell she was aching for me to eat her. I knew I was driving her wild, but to be honest I was just enjoying her so much I was in no hurry. I had also already cum and knew that lavishing some love on her would bring me back to full force again. And I was nearly there already anyway. I was a much more experienced lover these days and was determined to please this one.

With her arched the way she was and her jeans restricting her movement, I had free access to her pussy and arsehole. She was in what I call a tight doggie position with her jeans keeping her knees together. She was kind of trapped really. I could do anything I wanted. With her cheeks spread wide bent the way she was, I pulled her undies, which were stretchy green things that match her bra, over one cheek. That way I could access everything. She was such a sight at this point, arched back, arse in the air, pussy and anus on display. Her hair was completely covering her head, but I could hear her panting and whimpering with pleasure and anticipation. I started on her arsehole. It was so clean, sweet looking, and inviting. I felt I could lick it forever. The longer I spent on it, the more worked up I got. I was hard again now. My tongue darted in and out of her hole. She was in heaven. After this I came down finally to savour her pussy. She climaxed the moment I touched her lips. I then continued with her squealing so loudly I stopped at one point, thinking I might be in trouble with the noise.

She breathed heavily and asked, "What's the matter?"

"Nothing," I said. "Just checking you're all right."

"Yeah, don't stop. It's amazing."

I bathed my face in her at that angle for the next ten minutes. It was the perfect position to pleasure her orally, and I could have kept going for ages. Her arse was right at my face height, and I could just dive right in, no obstructions or awkward angles. She had climaxed multiple times by this point, and I thought it was time for her to meet the big boy. My cock was so hard by now I just positioned it in place, admiring the view of this perfect specimen momentarily, then thrust it straight in. She cried kind of painfully at first, and I thought, *Shit! I've gone a bit hard.* I backed off momentarily, but within a couple of seconds I was driving in fully and deep and slamming away hard. I couldn't really help myself. It just seemed like the way to go. I remembered Roni telling me to take my time, but sometimes slamming hard and fast just seemed right. After pumping her this way for quite a few minutes, I was ready to cum again. I could have held on as I had already cum, but feeling I'd given her a good go, I decided to let it go. I roared loudly, finally matching her noise. It was glorious.

I pulled out of her and collapsed on the couch. She had lay down in a kind of spoon position. We were both breathless and just stayed there recovering slowly. Estelle eventually got up and removed her jeans, asking if I'd like a drink. I asked for water. It was getting late, and I was feeling a bit awkward now, naked on her couch. I was thinking I should get going. It reminded me of the many one-night stands I'd had. She came back out naked with a glass of water. God, she was spectacular. She went and got a robe for herself and plonked down next to me on the couch. I'd covered my parts with a cushion, feeling a bit naked, and we both laughed after what we'd just done. It seemed silly. I don't know why I always felt a bit shy naked. We talked for a while. She snuggled into me lovingly. She had really enjoyed the encounter, but it was late and time for sleep. She said that any other night she would love me to stay, but she had an important early meeting. I said, "No probs," and got dressed and headed off. She wanted me to call her at work the next day. "Okay," I said and left. Wow, what a night. I was on fire! I enjoyed the drive home.

When I got home, it was late, and there was a note on my door saying that Angela had called and to call her back. It was way too late for that, so I went to sleep.

I was bugged the next day, getting up at around six thirty to get to work by seven thirty. I was feeling pretty good about myself even though I was tired. I would call Angela later in the day and of course Estelle. I couldn't wait. The other girls I was rooting had suddenly disappeared from my attention even though I enjoyed fucking every one of them. All I could think of for the moment was Estelle.

After work I called Estelle at her work. She was happy to hear from me. I could tell. It was mid-afternoon, and she invited me over again. "This time you can stay over," she said sexily. I had footy training and told her I would be there about nine o'clock. I hadn't quite worked out what I was going to do about Angela yet. I had a couple of hours to think about it and come up with something.

Angela had called the night before. When my housemate Mick got home, he told me she had called a couple of times wondering where I was. Mick knew that I was rooting around and was good at covering for me. That's what blokes did in these situations. We had been out picking up girls for years. Getting on the piss and chasing pussy was one of the things we lived for. I asked him what he told her, and he said he didn't know where I was; that was it. I thought, *Oh well, I'll have to make up something.* I called Angela before going to training and decided to tell her that I was feeling quite ill and had taken myself to the emergency department of the local hospital. It was okay. It turned out that as soon as I arrived there the problem passed. This was why I had missed her call, and it was too late by the time I got home. She was very concerned and demanded she come over after training to see me. I tried to put her off, but there was no stopping her. *Fuck it! What a jam*, I thought. I wanted to catch up with Estelle, and nothing was going to stop me. I headed off to training to try and figure it out.

After training I showered and dressed and then decided to ring Angela and tell her that a few of the guys were going out as a group bonding session and that I might be able to catch up a bit later. She wasn't happy but copped it, so I was free. I headed to Estelle's.

I got to Estelle's around nine as planned, and we fucked all night. We got a little bit of sleep, and I left for work at around 7:00 a.m., telling Estelle I would call later to see what she wanted to do.

I was tired that day at work, and all I wanted to do was finish and go home. I did notice this girl on a job that day in at a shop we cleaned regularly. She had a nice big rack and the type of arse that caught my eye. She seemed keen on me too, if a bit shy. If I wasn't so tired, I would have made a move. Another time, I thought. We finished around 1:00 p.m. as usual, and I went straight home to bed to sleep.

I woke to Angela around 6:00 p.m. She had called around to see me. I was dazed and tired from the lack of sleep I'd recently not had. I told her I was just recovering from the night before with the boys and apologised for not coming around. The night had become hectic, and I was still recovering. That's why I was crashed out. She bought it and suggested a night in with some takeaway and video. What could I do, really? I agreed and got up to take a shower to wake me properly. Somehow, I would have to ring Estelle. There was no way I was letting this hottie go. I would just have to tell her I was unavailable tonight and set up tomorrow. I thought, *Man this was getting difficult to manage.*

I was also wondering when I was going to get to my other girls next. I wanted them all and wasn't happy to let any of them go unattended for too long. I knew if I did that, they would get suspicious and realise I was rooting around and then they may not be interested in me. It was a predicament, and as usual I was thinking only of myself. What a guy! I had a lot on, including the following.

Roni: Although it was coming to an end, according to her, and it probably didn't matter.

Kim: She would need a visit asap.

Michelle: I cared about and was enjoying the sex.

Kasey: I had to see at least twice a week. We had sort of locked in Mondays and Tuesdays of late, and I wanted to keep that going. I loved the variety.

Belinda: Not really, but I did want to catch up with her and give her one. And I was certain I could if I could catch up with her. As long as I didn't bump into her biker boyfriend.

And of course, at the top of my list was Estelle. She was shiny and new and an absolute goddess. I just couldn't wait to get inside of her again.

And damn it, Angela was taking up more time. Not really, but I had to manage her carefully. She was my girlfriend, and I loved her. I also couldn't let her find out what I was up to, or she'd be devastated. The situation was challenging.

Angela and I drove to the shops, ordered some Chinese, and went to look at the videos. I didn't realise how distracted I must have been, but Angela did. She kept asking me what was wrong. And I kept lying and saying, "Nothing, why?" I tried to relax with her. I really enjoyed her company, and to be honest I was most comfortable with her out of all the women I was seeing. It was just the sex. I was having all this amazing sex with these other women and didn't enjoy sex with Angela. It was weird. *Why can't I just have such a good sex life with Angela and forget all these others and stop looking around for more?* I thought. I couldn't work it out and thought there was no solution. It's just the way it was. Even while at the video store, I couldn't help but check out the chick's arse who was serving us. I had noticed her every time I'd been in the store. Mark my housemate had as well, and we'd even talked about the first one to fuck her competition style.

When we got back, we ate our takeaway and settled on the couch to watch the video. I think it was *The Untouchables* with Kevin Costner. My attention was on the fact that I hadn't called Estelle and that she was expecting a call. We had also discussed me showing her around this weekend and even talked about going to the footy. She was interested in seeing me play. She was keen to be shown around by someone who knew the city, and I was that someone. Damn it! I suddenly said to Angela, "We should wait for the others, and they can watch the movie with us."

Angela was a little cool at the idea but agreed. I went to Mark's room. He was heading out shortly. I asked him to go and distract Angela while I made a phone call. "Diiiick!" said Mark, knowing I was up to no good. I begged him, so he did. He had a phone in his room, so I nervously called Estelle. When that sweet voice answered, I nearly just said, "I'll be over shortly," but I faked that I wasn't well and apologised, saying I'd give her a call tomorrow. She bought it and said she'd look forward to my call. Whew! I was good, I thought, at least until tomorrow. I re-joined Angela on the couch, and we enjoyed the movie together.

That night in bed Angela and I had a huge fight. It started with her wanting sex. We started, and I was more than obliging, but then she just stopped at one point and demanded I tell her what was going on. She could obviously tell that something wasn't right. I don't know how. Bloody women, moody as hell. How do they know these sorts of things? I told her nothing was going on. She questioned where I had been the other night when she called and didn't believe I'd gone to the hospital. Also, I never came around last night as planned. She knew I was up to something and thought I was seeing somebody else. She wanted to know the truth. I just kept on lying. I couldn't tell her the truth. She would freak. She was already freaking out right now, so how could I possibly tell her what was really going on. I couldn't, so I held the line that she was imagining things, and that there was nobody else, and that she was being just a bit crazy. Well, she didn't take any of my thoughts or comments well, and after the two of us screamed back and forth for a bit, she got up and left. She said, "Maybe we shouldn't even be seeing each other if it's going to be like this." She slammed the door on the way out. I followed her to the car, but it was no use. She was going. She drove off with a screech. *Fuck, what just happened? Crazy bitch. This relationship stuff is hard,* I thought. *Who needs a girlfriend? It's just not worth it.*

It was around midnight, and I was wide awake now. I thought about it for a moment and then headed off to Kim's. She was happy to see me. No problems there. She'd only just gone to bed, greeting me at her door in just her summer gown. Her gorgeous nakedness was fully on display through the open gown, her hair dishevelled from being in bed. She welcomed me in with open legs, and we had a beautiful session as usual, with nothing held back. She was just about the perfect sex machine. I loved our sessions. We both crashed out about 2:00 a.m.

I woke at around 9:00 a.m. as usual with Kim wanting some more. We played for a while, wrestling in bed, and then I began to smack her arse. She loved it. I hadn't ever done this sort of thing much before with anyone, but Kim liked it and told me most women liked a good smack on the arse. "It's an erogenous zone," she said.

I said, "What?" I didn't know what that meant, and she explained it.

With that now explained well, I started to smack her, softly at first, just playfully really, like she was a naughty little girl. Well, she liked it and liked it a lot. She kept encouraging me and moaning pleasurably until she had her arse high in the air and I was really whipping it. I turned her cheeks a nice red colour. My cock was so hard by this time you could drive a train along it. The action of smacking her arse was a real turn on, and I occasionally gave her a break for a quick lick and suck of her bits. Kim jerked my cock, and I forced it into her willing mouth, deep-throating her vigorously. After a bit of that I returned to her rear for some hard hits and then I fucked her doggie style until we both climaxed. I pulled out and shot my load onto her red raw arse. She lay there smiling, spreading my seaman over her arse cheeks almost like she was trying to repair the damage. "Man, that was fun," I told her. She agreed. We showered together and then I left. I had to get to the game.

My footy team were playing the top team today, and I needed to get my shit together. I was an important player, and the team depended on my performance or at least that's how I saw myself. As I drove to the game, I thought about what to do with Angela. I was pissed off about the night before and was really getting sick of her shit. I was thinking maybe I would be better off without her. I had never had that thought before, and I pondered it momentarily. It would certainly make it easier to have all these other women if I didn't have any commitment with just one. That was obvious, but how would I end it? I couldn't even begin to confront the idea. I was such a wimp in hindsight when I look back now. Better to just keep it going and not upset the apple cart as the saying goes. Fuck all this. I've got a game to play.

We played well and were winning at halftime. I was having a good game, but they overran us in the second half. They had a lot of really experienced senior players and were a big money club in the competition. They were basically buying themselves a premiership while we were a struggling local club.

Angela was in the rooms after the game and came up to me apologising for our fight. I was a bit indifferent, but I felt that same old commitment for our relationship that I'd always had and apologised as well, saying I was sorry for it as well. Fuck, now I had a real problem, as I wanted to see Estelle tonight. We had a few drinks at the club and then I told Angela that I was heading out with the boys tonight. She wasn't happy, but I told her I had already made these plans, as I didn't know she was coming down after last night. I also made up some more bullshit that I was playing golf the next day and that I'd come over tomorrow night. She wasn't happy, but she copped it given what had happened the night before. I felt bad because I could see she was sad that we weren't going to be together until tomorrow, but I had to get to Estelle. I was desperate to see her again, and I knew she was waiting to hear from me. We left the club with Angela going her way and me going mine. If she really knew what I was up to, the shit would hit the fan. I didn't care about that right now. All I wanted was to get with Estelle, the sooner the better.

Estelle answered. She was excited to hear from me I could tell. She was happy I was feeling better and keen for me to come around. I arrived at about 9:00 p.m., and she looked stunning. She was keen to go out and have a look around town. She hadn't done this since arriving as her job had kept her so busy. I suggested we walk around town and find somewhere to hang out, get some food, etc. She liked the idea, so that's what we did. We ended up down by the river, which she really enjoyed. I was just really enjoying her, holding her, grabbing her, groping her whenever I got the chance. It was great that we were already fucking; it made this time much more relaxing.

I had promised to show her around some sites of Melbourne and suggested we do that tomorrow. It would be great during the day to head down the coast. "I thought maybe we would head down the coast," I suggested, and she loved the idea. For now, though, we headed back to her apartment for another glorious night of sex. We did it all, eventually crashing out at about 3:00 a.m. We had a big day ahead, so we needed to sleep.

We woke at about 9:00 a.m. I fucked her doggie before having a shower and then heading down to a coastal hotel for lunch. When we got there, she caused quite a stir not only because she was so damn stunning that every man was checking her out but also because we met some people from her work. It was awkward for me, but she was fine. All the commotion made me nervous and had me wondering if anyone I knew would see me and blow my cover. Anyway, we had a nice lunch and checked out the beaches and headed back to town around 5:00 p.m. Talking on the way back, Estelle found out that I had a girlfriend. She wasn't upset. She knew what men were like she said and didn't care because I was a great fuck. I thanked her. This made me feel great. She did suggest I shouldn't do that and that I will break someone's heart.

She was right of course. I had been feeling more and more guilty lately about my treatment of Angela, but what could I do? I loved all this pussy I was getting. I didn't tell Estelle that there were any others, just that I loved fucking her as well and that we should keep at it if she wanted to. She smiled, sexily reached over, and squeezed my cock. "Of course."

We arrived back at her apartment around 7:00 p.m. We were both tired. She asked if I wanted to stay, and I told her that I wanted to but that I had promised the girlfriend I'd come over tonight. It felt good that I wasn't hiding this from Estelle. At least now I didn't have to lie to her as well; all these lies were hard to manage. Estelle wasn't making it easy to leave, though, teasing me about what I would be missing if I left. She started to do a bit of a show for me, touching herself, pointing her arse at me, bending over. Fuck, she was hot. "Fuck it," I said. "I won't stay the night but I'm going to give it to you before I go."

I gave the best oral performance I could muster. Hanging out with her all day and then finally coming home to her sexy show had driven me mad sexually and I was giving her my best. After pleasuring her orally and fingering her to multiple climaxes, I stood up and placed my cock in her mouth. She took it all, deep throating me as best she could until I came, and she swallowed it all. Fuck, we had some good dirty sex together. It looked like she'd been crying, but it was just that the deep throat action caused the tears to flow. She was also breathless afterwards as I had cum so intensely.

With that we said our goodbyes and planned to catch up soon. I said I would give her a call to her reply of "I look forward to it."

I loved that about Estelle. She reminded me of Kim, very similar, built for sex and lots of it. I headed to Angela's house. I drove fast to Angela's house and got pulled over by the cops. Damn it, cost me time and money. I arrived at Angela's at around 9:30 p.m., and the mood was cool. It was nice to see her. Like I have said before I felt more comfortable with her than any other woman. We were just not that compatible sexually. When I asked how she was, she said, "Fine. Are you staying?"

Let me tell you when a woman says she's fine, she's not fine! Even I could see that. I said, "Of course I'm staying."

"You don't have anywhere else you have to go?"

I copped it and admitted that I hadn't been around much lately, but she was the one that stormed out Friday night. Angela interrupted me, saying, "The girls here reckon you're sleeping around. Are you?"

I was floored. Fuck it! I must have looked like a deer in the spotlights too. I reckon because that's how I felt. I knew I didn't like these bitches she lived with, except Karen. Actually, I didn't like her either. I had secretly fantasised about her and had masturbated thinking of her a few times. One time I jerked off in the toilet at their place while I watched her putting clothes on the line. Angela had nicked out to the shops, and I could see Karen through the dunny window while I was taking a piss. Karen was late twenties, and I could tell she liked cock. There was just something sexual about her that I liked. She had a big mouth, and I always thought of stuffing my cock in there and that she would love it.

It turned out that Karen had been the one that put it in Angela's head that I was screwing around. Interestingly none of her housemates were there at the time. I guess they'd cleared out to avoid any unpleasantness. I assured Angela as sincerely as I could muster that I was not sleeping around and asked what made Karen and her think that. She gave me the silent treatment mostly, not answering my question, which was really making me angry. Fuck this, why couldn't all women just be like Estelle and Kim and Roni and Kasey and Michelle? They didn't give me any hassles. Jeez! I was angry with Karen. I told Angela she had no right to accuse me of this. Angela's silence only made me feel more like I was busted. I didn't really know what to say or do, so I said nothing, but inside I was a mess, and I was busted. I had a shower, and we went to bed; Angela noticed the scratches on my back. Both Kim and Estelle had had a go over the last forty-eight hours. I brushed it off as from the footy game. You always got scratches from playing footy, which was true. Angela was silent.

I headed off to work in the morning before Angela was awake fully. I gave her a kiss and whispered, "I love you," and I did.

It was Monday, and I was working with Bob. I loved working with him. We had a cool shop run on a Monday morning that ended at a great brekkie spot. I told Bob about my travails, and he laughed, mostly thinking, "Oh you poor bastard." He thought it was hilarious. "Most guys would love to be getting all the free pussy you're getting. Are you for real? Why don't you just come clean with your girlfriend and break it off?" he said. "You'll be better off, you and her."

It was sound advice when I look at it now. I mean, what I'd been doing was crazy. He said, "You're a young man. Go spread your wild oats. Get it out of your system, and if it's meant to be with Angela, she'll be there later if she's the one." That was Bob's advice, and I should have taken it. In the meantime, though he wanted all the gooey details, as he loved living vicariously through me, he said. He was married and used to root around as a young fella but wasn't interested in that anymore, and so his advice was probably sound. For some reason I couldn't do it, though. I was in love with Angela. I was just a gutless prick who wanted it all and didn't realise the consequences of my actions. I really had no idea. He loved the sound of all my girls and thought that I should enjoy them while I could because nothing lasts forever. I didn't believe him, though; I was just getting started.

That afternoon I called on Kasey. She worked the bar at an inner-city hotel near the university. She was alone and it wasn't busy, so she took me to the stock room and gave me a blowjob. Fuck, I loved this girl. What a dirty girl and pretty too. She demanded that I fuck her later, but I said I didn't know if I could. She said she'd come over to my place, which I wasn't keen on, but she was dying for my cock. She said she'd been dreaming of me. She begged. It's amazing to have a woman begging for your cock. I told her I needed to catch up with Michelle and she suggested that she'd come over as well. She'd be off at 5:00 p.m. We could fuck there. I said, "Are you crazy? We can't fuck at Michelle's!"

"Why not? She won't mind," Kasey said. It sounded weird to me, but I needed to see Michelle. I'd promised I'd come over at least once a week to see how she was doing, and I also liked fucking her. I left promising to catch up with Kasey tomorrow.

I fucked Michelle and was gone by 6:00 p.m. I headed to Angela's house. I needed to see how she was doing after last night. Her behaviour had been weird even though she was spot on. I was a cheating arsehole and had been throwing my cock all over town. I couldn't believe that they'd worked it out. Angela was happy to see me. Her mood was different. She apologised for her accusations and said that Karen and she were just talking about the possibility because that's one of the things that can happen when your boyfriend isn't around. I was relieved and pleased to be off the hook. Little did they know how spot on they were. I stayed the night, enjoying Angela's company. It was nice to be together.

The next day as promised I met Kasey after work and drove her home. I gave her my best performance. I knew I wouldn't be able to see her as often now so I thought I would just make every encounter the best I could. I didn't tell her this of course; I sensed she might not take it well. Get her to climax, fuck her in the arse, deep-throat her, finger her hard—she loved it all, the dirtier and harder the better. When we were done, I came out of the bedroom and Belinda was there. I thought, *Jeez she would have heard all that!* Not that it mattered. She knew us both.

She looked at me sexily and said, "When am I going to get another go?

I smiled and said, "Whenever you want." I walked over to her and gave her arse a squeeze. I really was hoping I would get a go at Belinda alone this time.

She just laughed and said, "I don't think I'll get a chance between Michelle, Kasey, and your girlfriend. What's her name?"

Her comments made me uneasy. I acted cool, though, or so I thought. "I bet she'd ditch you pretty quick if she knew what a scumbag cheater you are," Belinda said.

Kasey came in and said, "Maybe we should tell her!"

I was pissed inside at the thought. I knew these two could be trouble, not that I would let it happen. I was playing a dangerous game, however, especially with these two because they just didn't seem to care about anyone. They liked sex, that was obvious, but they didn't care about who they stood on to get it. That was my feel of these two. I did like the easy sex, though, and as usual that was my primary thought. I was also excited about the idea of fucking Belinda and thought I would tell her as much.

Kasey warned me, "Her boyfriend will bury you!"

I could tell that Belinda would like some, though. She enjoyed me as much as the others in the foursome. Anyhow it was time to leave so I told Kasey I'd call by again soon. She was sweet.

As I headed for my car, a guy on a motorbike rocked up. It was Belinda's boyfriend, the one I'd been warned about. He gave me a foul look, challenging me, but I just kept going, hopped in my car, and left. *That was close*, I thought, and he didn't look friendly so best to avoid him for everyone's sake.

When I got home, I called Angela and invited her over. I thought it would be a good idea to keep it rolling and see her as much as I could. Plus I was missing her. She couldn't come, though. The girls were having some kind of party plan. I also called Estelle. I was missing her. She was very hard to get out of my mind. I'd been crazy busy since seeing her on the weekend, but she was cool and was keen to see me whenever I was available. I told her I wasn't sure when as I needed an early night, but I would call her at work tomorrow to see what she was up to.

The next day I called in on Roni at about 11:00 a.m. I was working alone and near her house, so I thought what the heck, I'd see what she was doing. She was pleased to see me and invited me right in. She made a cuppa tea for us both and we chatted. When we finished, I asked her if she'd like me to rip off her pantyhose. She did of course, so I started by fingering her after ripping her hose, first with one finger and adding more as she heated up and lost control. I ripped open her top to release her tits, sucking and chewing on them while fingering her vigorously. After making her climax, she sucked me off, swallowing it all. She was a real pro. I loved cuming this way in a woman. It just felt so wrong and so right. Roni mentioned that this could be our last time and it was probably for the best really. I didn't need it from her anymore because I was getting so much, although she was a great fuck. I also enjoyed her grace and experience. She really knew how to treat my cock, so I would miss this. It was also nice to know I could call in if the mood took me. It was just superb that I could offer this service to the local lonely housewives. Dick Pane to the rescue.

GETTING HER BOND BACK

APRIL 1985

In early April I was working with Peter. We had finished our shops and were now looking at a block of flats. This was a standard procedure at the company. We were meant to clean the flats, all external and internal of the entrance area, but we often just drove around it to see how dirty it looked. If it weren't too bad, we would just tick it off on the job sheet and go to the next job. Interestingly on this occasion we got busted. One of the residents had observed us driving around and not even getting out and wanted us to come back. The boss was a bit pissed when we got back because it obviously didn't look good and the last thing he wanted was to start losing work due to dodgy employee practices, even though he encouraged the practice if we could get away with it. His first line to me when I started was "You don't clean a clean window."

That said, he didn't like it when we got caught out and so we needed to go back and fix it ASAP.

Peter was in a bit of a huff. He needed to head off early for some reason so I just said I would go back and fix it, no worries. It was still early anyway and one of those beautiful sunny autumn days. I loved the weather this time of year. It was warm relaxing, not too hot but beautiful in the sun. I headed back on my own in the work vehicle to take care of it.

When I got to the flats, I took the ladder off the roof and got stuck into the job. I'd only just started when this lady came out and questioned me about why we had driven off. I told her we thought that another crew had already done them because they looked so clean. She looked at me funny and said, "Wait until you see mine." I agreed that we'd made a mistake and told her not to worry, I'd take care of them. She disappeared momentarily but then returned and asked me if I would be interested in doing her inside windows. I told her we were just doing the outsides. She said that she would make it worth my while and that she would be happy to work something out. She needed them done because they were filthy, and she wanted to get her bond back. I wasn't really interested but the thought of a little extra cash and something about the way she pleaded got me agreeing. I told her I'd finish the outside first and then come and see her.

Crazy women, they just love getting their windows cleaned. I'd never cleaned my own windows in my life and in fact never even realised this would be a real job until I came across it in the Saturday paper that day. I also couldn't believe how much money people paid to have their windows cleaned. The wealthy clients we did work for paid top dollar. Money wasn't a problem and the boss's business was making heaps.

When I got to the back of the flats, each unit had a private backyard that was fenced off. This wasn't unusual. Lots of flats and apartments were like this. Blocks like this are just a bit more difficult to complete. You have to lift the ladder over each fence to get the high windows in every courtyard and then jump over each fence with the bucket and your gear. It took a bit of energy and was a bit of a hassle but seeing we were already busted on this job I just had to suck it up and do it.

When I was up the ladder in the second backyard, I noticed a lady in a pink bikini lying on a banana lounger in the next backyard. I had a bit of a perve when I realised. She looked like her eyes were shut and was totally relaxing, unaware of me. She certainly didn't seem to have any attention on me. This was interesting, as in a minute I would be crashing over the fence unannounced. This was one of the hazards of the job because sometimes people would get shitty at the way we just jump into their backyards. There wasn't really any other way, however, until someone came up with a better system.

Knowing this lady was there I poked my head over the fence first and announced myself, telling her I was the window cleaner.

She responded with "Yeah, that's fine. Just go ahead."

She surprised me because I hadn't noticed that it was the same lady who I had met around the front. Wow, she now just had a pink string bikini on and was pretty sexy. She had a great body. She was older, probably in her forties, with blonde straight hair. She was hot, very fuckable by my estimation. I hadn't taken too much notice of her out the front because she seemed a bit plain at first in a tracksuit and I really wasn't expecting anything like this. I was quite flustered now because I was now really interested in this woman for the purposes of sex.

She asked me if she was in the way, to which I said, "No I'll manage." She reckoned she wanted to catch the last bit of sun before winter and that also she was moving to the Gold Coast and didn't want to go up there looking lily white. I took my chance and I told her there was no problems there and that she looked great. She liked that. I could tell, and I think she could tell that I liked looking at her. I thought I would make it obvious. What the fuck, why not? I could feel another potential fuck coming on. *Okay*, so I thought, *let's see where this goes.* This was starting to look very interesting! I finished her outside upstairs windows, perving as I did them, using the glass reflection to good use. I noticed that she was watching me also, probably checking out my arse. Ladies always did. I slid down the ladder sailor style, putting on a bit of a show for her, and then put the ladder over the fence.

She gasped, "Gee, you're good at that." I was thinking now I couldn't wait to do the insides. There was definitely an opportunity here. I mean who does that? She knew I was coming around the back and she's laying on a banana lounger in a bikini, oiled up too. Yeah, that's right. She was oiled up as well. Her skin was all shiny. I couldn't believe this. I'd found a live one here. I was processing so much of this information in a short period of time and all nerves led to my penis. She had gotten out of her tracksuit she had on when I met her out front and was now in this. Wow! *She's fucking with me, and she wants some*, I reckoned. *Nothing else makes sense.* I thought to myself, *Let's get these outsides done and get back to do her inside windows and see where this goes.*

As I went to get over the fence I heard, "You can do my inside windows now." This stopped me and I turned to see her get up out of the lounger. As she did, I got an eyeful of her snatch with her legs spread and she looked great. She had a nice figure in good shape and nice size tits. I would love to fuck this dirty old tease. She was really putting on a show. There was no doubting it. I was being flirted with no doubt and my penis was starting to react. She tiptoed over to her sliding back door and opened it for me, motioning me in.

As I grabbed my bucket and went inside, she smiled and then apologised for the mess her house was in, but it didn't bother me. She started picking stuff up, bending over and giving me a great view of her arse and pussy. Also her tits were bouncing around, which was very enjoyable to watch. I just stopped and stared. She was a mature woman, but her body was great and in that little bikini I was really getting a great look at her and aroused. She turned and noticed me staring, so I pulled myself together and told her I would get started upstairs.

As I headed up, she told me to just move anything that was in the way. I turned to check her out as I got to the top of the stairs only to see that she was doing the same, checking me out. The way she was looking at me, she wanted it.

Fuck, I couldn't believe my luck. This was great. My cock was really starting to stir now with the anticipation. I gave it a squeeze and it felt nice. I heard her sliding door open and close and could see she was back outside. She started to put more suntan oil on, and I just perved at her from her bedroom window. Fuck, this was a horny situation to be in. I started cleaning her windows, and it was obvious I was sure she knew that I could see her. She was really putting on a show as well, standing and wiping the oil over her arms, arching her back to really show off her figure to me. At least that's what it looked like she was doing. A second later she was back laying sexily on the banana lounger. I had been holding and rubbing my cock through my shorts while watching her and the thought did go through my head that I could just jerk off while watching her.

I noticed her bedside drawer was open and I could see some undies. All of this was becoming too much; I was in a bother. I was as horny as hell. This bitch was really getting me going, but I had no idea what to do about it. I had to let her make the first move. I mean, there was something not right about being in someone's home who you are there to do a window cleaning job for and making the first move, especially in a sexual sense. You know what I mean. It just wouldn't be right. What if she was just a tease and if I made a move, then

I could be in trouble. No, I would have to let her make a move until I was sure. I was nervous and excited. I had to let this play out, but I could only follow her lead. My cock was also quite hard now. I couldn't see me getting rid of it unless I blew. I could just jerk off quickly and then be on my way, but it would probably take too long. I was really contemplating it when I noticed a big rubber cock vibrator on the floor next to her bed. I picked it up and held it next to my bulging cock, pressing out against my shorts. Wow, she can take a bit it seemed, if this rubber cock was anything to go by. Fuck, this was too much, I thought. I decided then that I needed to get a move on. She would soon become suspicious as to what I was doing up there. I couldn't jerk off there even though I knew I would cum quickly. It was just too risky, and what was I thinking anyway? I was turning into a real devo.

I pulled myself together, stopped perving on her and touching myself, and finished the windows upstairs. My cock had settled down to a respectable level and I repositioned it in my shorts so it wasn't too obvious, then headed downstairs. As I started to clean the kitchen window that looked out onto her sunbathing, she got up and came to the sliding door, opening it and thanking me saying, "This is so going to help me get my bond back."

I was like putty in her hand at this point and just said, "Sure."

I just wanted to fuck this woman. I was so turned on and trying to control myself with some deep breathing. There's something about standing as a stranger in a woman's home when she is wearing only a bikini that just makes you want to fuck. The little tease had deliberately set this situation up and she knew I was wanting her.

She then asked me what she owed for the job. I said we would normally charge about $35 for this, as that was our company's minimum. I really didn't care about some cash at this point. I was just so turned on to be in the presence of this bikini-clad woman. The stimulation was payment enough. I was hoping for something else.

She was like, "Oh god that much. I'm just trying to get my bond back. We really don't have to involve the company, do we? I must pay you something, though. You're doing a great job. Let me check if I have any money upstairs."

She headed upstairs. Wow, she was really bunging on her financial dilemma. As I finished off the sliding glass doors, I could feel her watching me from behind. She was checking me out. I knew she would be enjoying my arse and probably my back wheels from her angle. Many women had admired and commented on my body over time. I knew she would be no different, especially after her behaviour and display.

I turned and said, "Well, that's it" and started to move outside when it happened.

She said, "Well, I have to pay you something but I'm so tight for money as the move is so expensive. Can we work something out? What can I do for you?"

A bit confused, I said, "What do you mean? I hadn't picked up on her cue, but then I did.

She then said, "I could pay you some other way," and looked at me suggestively and kept moaning. "It's just that money is so tight at the moment."

At that point I was like, *Yeah, okay, fuck it.* "Look, you're sexy and I hope you won't be offended but if I'm going to be honest, I'd love to fuck you."

She paused momentarily, mouth open, pretending to be shocked, but she loved it. I couldn't believe I'd come out with it and then she just laughed sexily and said, "Well, no! You can't fuck me, not for a $35 job. I'm not that cheap." She sounded all indignant like I had insulted her. "I'll give you a hand job"

I put the bucket down and stood facing her and just said, "Fuck yeah!" What a dirty little old slut, I thought, just my type of woman. I was so proud of myself at that point. I loved that this was where we were at, and she liked it as well.

She said, "Let's do it upstairs."

"Yeah, okay." Walking towards her I just wanted to grab her, throw her down, and fuck her hard, the dirty little bitch. I thought about Kim and the fantasies she had about being raped by an intruder. At this point I was just so excited I was going to get my cock jerked by this stranger and who knew, I'd probably fuck her. I was totally turned on. My cock was starting to grow, bulging in my shorts. As I followed her upstairs, I couldn't help myself. I grabbed at her arse. It was nice and soft. Fuck, I was horny now.

I went to grab her again as we entered her bedroom, but she stopped me, saying, "No!" quite firmly. It stopped me in my tracks. "I'm only going to jerk you off, that's all."

It was funny, and I said, "Okay, sure." What else could I say? It still sounded pretty good to me.

She laid down a towel on the bed and said, "We'll do it here." It was funny in a way, quite clinical, but who cared, I was about to get my rocks off. She wanted me to cum on the towel. Before we began, she told me she loved the sight of my cock bulging in my shorts. I was speechless and just gawked back at her as she reached forward and squeezed my cock through my shorts.

I moaned. "Yeah!" And before I could do or say anything, she had unbuttoned my footy shorts and pulled them down, releasing my cock with a snap. My wallet fell to the floor with a thud. Kneeling, she had my cock and balls in her hands, and she started to jerk. I was so hard and fully erect within a few pulls and she gave it a good dry tug. She told me she loved a big, long, hard cock and that I had a nice one. I just stood there looking down at her while she jerked away and then she started to suck on it. This was great a bonus. I was enjoying this obviously and started to touch her hair and then reached down for a handful of breast.

She stopped sucking at my grope and told me, "No, stop it." She moved back and slapped my cock hard.

Fuck, that hurt and I was like, "What the fuck!"

She stood up and said, "No touching."

"Okay, but hang on, you started sucking my cock. What did you expect?"

"Well, I like your cock. It looks nice. If I want to suck on it while I jerk it, that's up to me. How else do you expect me to get it lubricated?"

It was a fair point. It had been a bit of a rough dry jerk up until then, but I didn't mind. I liked it pulled dry or any which way. She then said, "If you want any more, then you will be paying me money." Interesting thought. This was a bit of a switch up.

I knew I had around $5 in my wallet so I said, "I got $5. What can we do?"

She was like, "Forget it! I'm giving you a hand job and then were done, that's it." Spitting on her hand, she resumed stroking while standing next to me, pulling my cock toward the towel. She then pressed right against me, right arm around my waist, jerking me with her left. I was stiffening again and with her hand and my cock now quite wet from saliva and a bit of my precum it was feeling nice. She was stroking me from base to head, giving it just the right amount of pull in the middle. She had done this before. She was masterful at this and in my state, I wasn't going to last long. Pressed beside me, she could tell this from my breathing and moans. I stared down at her tits, breathing heavily. I asked her if I could see her tits and she started licking and sucking on my nipple.

"Show me your tits," I pleaded as I tried to keep control. She stopped momentarily and pulled her bikini top aside, releasing a beautiful pair of melons. I was like, "Let me suck on them."

She said, "No."

"But they're beautiful," I pleaded, "and it'll make me come quicker," to which she finally gave in. I began to lavish some love on those beautiful things, grabbing them with both hands, squeezing gently and sucking and licking her nips. She moaned pleasurably while still jerking me. She wanted to get this done. I was telling her how sexy she was while I moaned with pleasure as she jerked away and that I'd really like to lick her pussy, telling her how nice it would be, but that was it. She moved me back and knelt in front of me, then started really jerking me to a finish. She had her head right against me, licking and sucking my balls. She started talking dirty too, saying she loved having a big hard long cock in her hands and having cum all over her. She sucked my cock a few more times, alternating between hand and mouth until eventually I was about to burst.

"Cum on my tits. C'mon, I know you're going to cum. Cum all over them." With her hands sliding over my cock and talking the way she was, I came a big load all over her tits, tummy, and even her legs. It was a big mess and that's where she directed it. I grunted loudly, convulsing as she pulled it all out. I couldn't care who heard. She was quite experienced. What a dirty bitch. I loved it. It was like she was milking a cow. She pulled and squeezed my cock that hard, especially at the end, wanting to get every little bit of spunk I had. She was looking quite impressed with herself too. She told me she loved being cum on by a good-looking stranger with a big cock like mine. Jeez, she loved the dirty talk and so did I.

She reached for the towel, standing up and wiping herself down. There was a bit to clean up and I watched as she wiped herself dry of my cum. I was breathless and wanting to sit down. I headed toward a chair in the corner. She piped up sharply, "Don't sit down! We're done, and I want that $5." I watched her put her tits away and I picked up my wallet.

I pulled out a $5 note, handing it to her and smiling. "Thanks for that. That was grouse." I would love to have done more and even had another go at her while standing there with my shorts down, cock swinging in the breeze.

She said, "C'mon, time to go."

Wow, she's not so nice now, dirty little cow, I thought.

"I just need to get my bond back," she repeated.

With that I pulled up my shorts and put my cock away. Out of curiosity I asked her as I was leaving, "If I paid her some more money, could we have another go and this time do a bit more?"

She was interested! She asked me what I wanted to do, standing there looking sexy with her hands on her hips. I looked her up and down smiling and said, "Everything, you know, just go at it, no holds barred. You can even slap my cock again if you like." It had kind of felt nice. "As long as I can slap your arse, the works."

She asked me what I would pay, and I said, "How about $25?"

To that she didn't even hesitate, saying if I bought her back $50 today I could do whatever I liked. That was it. "Deal." I told her I'd finish up the windows, hoping over her fence, and that I'd be back in about an hour. I returned as planned and spent a good hour fucking. She was a great fuck, that's what I thought about her. Like she said she needed to get her bond back and I wanted to get my money's worth. It did annoy me a bit that I had paid for sex but the encounter with her was just so dirty and different, something not right, that I couldn't resist. It was a great session as well. I really gave her a good banging and she liked it as well. She was woman enough to handle anything I did to her.

FROM THE JOURNAL

Got jerked off by this mature bikini babe today while cleaning windows at a block of flats. She wanted her inside windows cleaned and she was a total tease and wanted fucking. I was so turned on by this woman she totally played me. She cried poor after the job was done and offered me a hand job instead of money for payment. I suggested we fuck instead. It's the boldest play by me to date and it worked. Well, I got a hand job. After a great hand job that turned into her sucking me off as well as me blowing on her tits. I also got to play with her tits during this. We did it upstairs in her bedroom. She laid a towel on the bed initially for me to cum on, but she ended up jerking me all over her in her tits. She talked dirty too and told me she loved having a big hard long cock in her hands and having cum all over her. When we were done, I asked if I paid more could I fuck her, to which she agreed. I came back an hour later and spent a good hour fucking her. It cost me $50, which sucks, but it was something different and another window cleaning adventure. Fuck yeah! Ha ha, I did my part

FROM THEN ON

To this day it remains as one of the most surprisingly erotic moments I have experienced. I really enjoyed just being jerked off. All I had to do was just stand there and supply my cock. The way she spoke while doing it was a real turn on. To be jerked off by a total stranger while on the job was a new one to me at the time. As I was to find out, however, the "being fucked by a stranger" fantasy is a popular one for women and I had some more to come, ha ha.

When I got home that night, I told my housemate Mark what had happened. He thought it was a classic and wondered how he could perhaps knock on her door by accident and see if he could get some. We laughed and thought maybe pretend to be doing a survey on women who like being cum on by big, long, hard cocks. Fuck, we had a good laugh. He couldn't believe the run of sex I was getting and for that matter neither could I. He was pretty good with the ladies himself, standing six feet four and being a gentle giant. The girls loved him. I can't remember him not having a girlfriend and he had had a few.

BEING DUMPED

When I spoke to Angela on the phone, she sounded unhappy. She wanted me to come over as she had something to tell me. When I got to her house, the other bitches were there. I wasn't really getting along with any of them at this point as I was still pissed about Karen for suggesting that I had been screwing around. Angela's mood was dire. I could tell something big was coming but was still shocked when she suggested we break up. I stood there stunned for a moment in shock and then asked why. What was wrong? I wondered.

I was such an idiot. I had been so caught up in myself for the past so many months that I had no idea how I'd been mistreating Angela. She told me how unhappy she was that I never really wanted to have sex with her or showed any interest in her at all. We never talked. We had no plans, and she was just sick of it. This was all correct of course, as I had been spending so much time screwing around, there was no time at all to create a relationship. Still, I was devastated, and I suggested we give it another go. Angela wouldn't have it. She wanted a break and that was that. I got angry at that point and accused her housemates of filling her head with lies about me and of course with them in the background, how could we possibly have a relationship? It was pathetic really; I was a dirty rotten cheater, and I knew it, but I just wasn't ready to let Angela go. I loved her. What had I done? Once I settled down, we both took turns in crying until I eventually left into the cold night. It was midnight as I was driving home, and I was feeling pretty low. I was genuinely heartbroken by Angela's decision to end it. I'm sure I was in shock. I felt physically ill. Still, before I knew it, I was parked out front of Kim's flat, rain pelting down to match my mood. I went inside and fucked her hard. It had been a while since I'd seen her, but she didn't mind. In fact she was dying for it and questioned me about where I had been for the last couple of weeks. I told her I'd just been busy with family and stuff, and she left it alone.

The next day at work I was sombre, still devastated really and a little lost. I felt like I had a hole in my heart. I carried on as normal, though, I didn't want to discuss it with anyone there. The blokes at work wouldn't care anyway and what right would I have for complaining anyway. For the rest of the week, I just worked and stayed home. I called Angela a couple of times and we spoke briefly, but she was adamant it was over. Her calendar was full of activities that didn't include me. I was a fool, and I was heartbroken.

On Saturday night after football, I called Estelle and told her I had broken up with Angela. She was going to a party and invited me along. I met her at about 10:00 p.m. She looked stunning in tightest jeans in history. We got to the party not long after that and had a good time together. All the guys at this party were rich bastards from the advertising world, professional types of the sort I don't usually feel comfortable around, but this night I didn't care. I was with Estelle, and they were all jealous, and I think my fuck-you attitude came from the fact that I was missing Angela. I spent the rest of the weekend with Estelle. It was nice to have company that helped me forget about Angela and of course fucking her was a treat. When I was heading off on Monday morning to work, she suggested that I should move into her apartment. It took me by surprise, and I told her that I would ring her after work, as I didn't have time right now to discuss.

When I finished around 2:00 p.m., I called Estelle at her work, and she invited me over for dinner. I thought, *Why not? I don't have to be anywhere anymore. I'm not hiding anything.* It felt good. She would be home at 7:00 p.m. These advertising execs worked long hours I thought, or was it just that window cleaners worked short hours. Obviously it was a bit of both.

I had a bit of time on my hands so decided to drop in on Kasey at the pub thinking that I might be able to get her to blow me again in the stock room as I had really enjoyed that last time. Unfortunately, the pub was busy and there were other staff on, so I had to settle for a crude grope at the end of the bar. Neither of us minded that. I was thinking, *Oh well, I'll call on Michelle*. I didn't tell Kasey, however, as I knew she wanted me the moment I walked in. I was also keen to get with her as the sight and feel of her arse had made me want her bad. I really enjoyed fucking her. She was crazy in bed and a real dirty girl. As I left, I decided to appease her by saying I would come over to her house tomorrow. She said it couldn't happen and that Belinda's boyfriend was staying a lot lately and he wouldn't want me around her. I didn't like the sound of him either so suggested she come over to my house. She was surprised and asked, "Why the change?" I didn't say. I just gave her my phone number and told her to call when she knocked off.

I headed to Michelle's and arrived around 4:00 p.m. It was nice to see her. She was also happy to see me, and I told her I'd broken up with Angela. She was surprised and curious if I was okay and we discussed what had happened over a couple of drinks. After some advice from her we fucked on the couch. It was nice as usual and then I left to have dinner at Estelle's.

When I got to Estelle's, I needed a shower. I stunk from working that day and I'm sure that the smell of sex with Michelle was on me. I could smell her when I took a piss. I told Estelle I just needed a shower because of work, and she was cool. She made us some dinner. It was some kind of creamy pasta, bloody nice. Damn, this woman was amazing. There was a reason she wanted me to move in as it turned out. She was going to be heading back home to Hawaii in a month. It wasn't a total surprise as she had mentioned it before. The reason she wanted me to move in was just because she had been enjoying my company so much and the sex and she wanted to get as much of both before she headed off. She wasn't sure what the future held. She had thought since I'd broken up with Angela it might be possible to play life like a married couple for a time. I kind of agreed, as I was quite infatuated with Estelle. She was the most beautiful woman I had ever seen, and I enjoyed her completely.

I agreed to bring some stuff around and stay more often until she left but qualified it with saying that I'd have to train a couple of nights a week and that I couldn't move out completely as I'd need a place when she left. She was happy with that, and we had crazy sex that night. I worked on her for quite a while, licking her to multiple orgasms. I fucked her furiously when I got inside her. The fact that I'd fucked Michelle earlier just made me not want to cum. My cock stayed hard forever. My cock was so big and hard that night, I just enjoyed pounding away in every position I could throw Estelle. Man, she was awesome and so was I.

I could have happily spent the rest of my life with Estelle, but I was also lonely without Angela and constantly my thoughts turned to her. Even though I wasn't going without—regular intimate company with multiple women and all this company kept my mind off my breakup. Saying that, though, I still felt ill at times when I thought about Angela. Whenever I thought of her, I felt sad. I was worried about her. I wondered if she was okay. What was she doing? Was she happy? Underneath all my pathetic behaviour was a pathetic broken young man, really. In fact, in many ways I was still just an immature boy. I didn't know it back then, but I was lost in life. I had no idea about life and the damage I was doing to myself and others with my behaviour.

The very next day I let Kasey come over as promised. She had rung after work, and I had no reason to say no. Truth be known I really liked fucking her. She was a real sexual creature and the fact that she wanted me so badly made me want her also. I had also had trouble finding a place to fuck her for ages so getting her in my own bed with no guilt was amazing. We went at it till late in the morning and I ended up leaving her to go to work the next day. I had told her to call me whenever and we'd get together again. She didn't seem to mind, and I didn't really care if she did. We kind of had this agreement that we would fuck whenever we could; it suited us both.

I rang Estelle after work and told her I was going home to grab some stuff and that I'd be over tonight. She was rapt. For the next month until she left, I stayed there four to five nights a week. She visited the football club a couple of times and came to a few functions, causing a bit of a stir with the guys, as was her beauty. The local girls didn't like her either as every guy at the club was into her or wanted to be into her. She was only into me, though, and together for the month we both fell in love. It was sad when she left May 13. I'll never forget. We were both quite sombre as I drove her to the airport. She had suggested that I come out there to live. I could find work as a window cleaner if I wanted or something else. We both knew that it wouldn't happen and that it was probably for the best. Our worlds were vastly different and even though we had both enjoyed each other since meeting, it was never destined to last. She belonged with a billionaire. It was only a matter of time, and I was a Bogan from the southern suburbs, a window cleaner for fuck sake. We held each other tightly before she went through the departure gates. I never saw her or spoke to her again. I called her a couple of times, but it went nowhere.

It was for the best in a way as I was now freed up a lot to sniff around and get with some of my other girls. Over the next week I called on Michelle and Kim and had Kasey over a couple of nights. All of them were fine with my schedule except Kim hadn't seen me in a while and wondered where I'd been. I promised I wouldn't neglect her in future.

Michelle was heading off to Sydney that week and she had a bit of a send-off at her apartment. I rocked up with Mark my housemate and Kasey was over straightaway. Her eyes were all sex as usual, and I could see she'd be coming home with me. Belinda was there as well. It was nice to see her round arse. She was sexy, and I still wanted another go at her, this time alone. It was in the back of my mind and had been for a while. Michelle was cool towards me and understandably as it turned out; her ex was there. I talked with him for a while. If only he knew what I'd been up to. Oh well. Mark was getting on well with Belinda and I was a bit pissed that he was going to fuck her. I mean, she was my girl or kind of. Anyway I left him with her for ten minutes as I got Kasey to give me a blowjob outside in the pool area. Fuck, she was grouse. At the end of the night we left. I wished Michelle the best and that was the last time I ever saw her. Kasey was dropping Belinda home first and then coming over and as it turned out Mark and Belinda had gotten on very well. When I was getting blown by the pool, Mark was getting the same in the bathroom. "You lucky fucker," I told him. I'd been trying to get back into her since the first time. She couldn't come around with Kasey because of her psycho biker boyfriend but that didn't stop her giving Mark a blowjob, and from all accounts it was grand. A good night was had by all.

That following week I noticed that I wasn't missing Angela anymore or not as much anyway. I wrote it in my journal. It surprised me so much that even though my feelings had been strong to get back with her, I had still not done anything about it, and perhaps it was for the better. It was late May and I had lost three girls in the last month: Angela, Estelle, and now Michelle. This left me with much more time to fuck Kim and Kasey, though, and I alternated at will whatever I liked I got. I just rocked up at Kim's whenever and the same with Kasey, either at her work in the stockroom (Monday and Tuesdays were always quiet) or she'd come over when I let her. I really loved fucking her in the stockroom at the pub. There was this element of excitement that added to it. I would just sit her up on the rice bags and just slam it in her, with legs spread wide, I'd press back hard, pumping until I'd cum, usually bringing her forward to swallow my load or covering her in cum. She loved it. Sometimes I just came on her work gear and then we'd laugh while I had a drink and she served other customers with the jizz stains still on her uniform. We were both a bit perverted like that.

SHE WORKED IN RETAIL

LATE MAY

Layla

I was working with Wayne one day, doing the usual shop run, when I had my encounter with Layla. I had noticed her before a couple of times. She always seemed very businesslike towards us and not the type who would do what we ended up doing. What I had first noticed about her was her large tits, though. She wasn't much older than me and I usually checked her out but didn't think she had noticed. I had been enjoying perving on Layla the previous weeks and sensed an opportunity. There were also usually about three ladies in this shop as well but on this occasion only her and one other. It was a fancy women's clothes shop and had windows onto a main road at the front and some around the back to the car park. The shop was quite long, and we would split up to do the windows front and rear. On this occasion I went in to go to the rear windows while Wayne did the front. After that we would usually continue down in this fashion as many of the shops we did had front and rear glass. I would meet up with Wayne a bit later.

Because I walked through the shop, Layla had to unlock the rear door to let me get outside. I followed her to the rear of the shop, and I was having a good perv as she was quite curvy, and her arse had a real wobble that caught my attention. Her tits were large and lovely to look at also, so I always enjoyed this part of the job. To unlock the door, she had to squat down, which gave me a good look at her arse and had me fantasising at what might be with this beautiful peach. She was struggling to unlock the ground bolt as was sometimes common with this sort of mechanism. You had to have it lined up just right or it could be difficult to unbolt. She was really struggling so I put my bucket down and moved in to assist her, being the caring gentleman that I was. Just as I did that, she stood up quickly and we collided in the most spectacular way. I ended up with one hand on her large breast and the other with a handful of peachy soft arse, holding her from falling over.

I went to apologise as it had happened so fast but before I could really move away, she was wrapping herself around me. She turned, and our eyes locked, and that was it: we were involved in the most passionate of kisses and I was all in. She was all over me also, kissing passionately and feeling my arms and body, so I returned fire. I grabbed her arse and breasts and had a good feel all while sucking on her mouth furiously matching her energy. I started to suck on her neck, and it felt like she was going to climax right there. I was also getting hard quite quickly and the intensity of the moment was crazy. I pressed my cock hard against her. What the fuck, I thought; if she wanted a bit of a tussle, I'd give one.

She grabbed me by my shirt and led me quickly into a change room. Both of us looked towards the front of the shop to see if anyone had noticed. It was intense. The other girl was down the front of the store, and I was thinking she could discover us at any time but that didn't seem to matter right now as we were both breathing so heavy, and the privacy of the changeroom led me to dive into her tits. I pulled on her buttons, and it revealed the most amazing pair of breasts. Her soft lacy bra just stretched away as I sucked, licked, and nibbled all over them, stopping to pay attention to her nipples, which were large and hard and demanding attention. I cupped both breasts. They were a handful. I squeezed them together and licked furiously at her nipples. She groaned with pleasure. While bathing in her tits I could feel the intense pleasure of her grabbing and jerking at my cock through my shorts. It felt great. I was hard and ready to let it out.

My hand shifted up between her legs, pushing past her panties and feeling her warm wetness. I had two fingers in her going hard. She squealed and bit my shoulder as she was climaxing. It hurt me and made me force her back into the wall firmly. She was breathing heavily and slumped onto the small stool in the room, here beautiful tits exposed, panting and looking up at me. She was so hot for a fucking but there was no time for that. Also we could be discovered at any time, I kept thinking. Like a naughty schoolkid, I felt like I was committing some serious mischief and I could really get in trouble. My cock was so erect it was pressing so hard in my shorts and poking out the top. She looked at it and put her mouth over it, kissing and begging to take it inside her. I unsnapped my shorts, releasing it in a second. It sprang to attention, swinging upward and sideways right in front of her face, and she was on it. She swallowed it furiously, sucking like we had kissed and within about a minute I was done, ejaculating hard and intensely. She just took it all, sucking it up. I really gyrated as I climaxed, and it was quite violent for her as I pumped the last bits out. I muffled my climax as much as I could, but I couldn't believe that the other girl in the store wouldn't have noticed.

I stood there for a moment catching my breath. I straightened myself up as much as I could, my cock still fat from the exercise. She was also putting herself back together, tucking those huge tits away and buttoning up, also fixing her hair, which was a mess now. She looked like someone had just fucked her. We looked at each other and laughed quietly. I said, "Hi there, I'm Dick."

"I'm Layla."

"Well, we better get back to work. Let me get that door open." I peeked out of the changeroom, and it was clear the other girl was still busy down front and totally unaware of what had just happened. Layla squatted again and unlocked the door, then turned and smiled and walked away. I busily cleaned the outside window, realising I was now behind, and Wayne would be wondering where I was. Just as I was finishing Layla came to the door and handed me a piece of paper with her phone number. She smiled as I stuck it in my sock, and I went on my way.

FROM THE JOURNAL

Today I got a sensational surprise blowjob from the chick in this fancy ladies' clothing shop. I fingered her as well. It was a total surprise and totally awesome. She is quite sexy, and we just did it in a changing room all while another woman was working down the front. She got me so hard so quick I came in her mouth in about a minute and then I left with her phone number and continued with my day.

FROM THEN ON

Layla and I met many times outside her work after the initial encounter. She shared a flat with another girl and I would visit late afternoons and early evenings, usually straight after she would get home. Often, I would be waiting in my car as she got home. We would enter her home without too much talking, and I would just take her straight to her bedroom. I always fucked her dominantly. I loved it that way with her and so did she. I always had rough sex with her and as soon as we would catch up, I would grab her and start groping and getting at it. I loved to smack her arse hard and her tits, and she liked it too. I would hit that thing so hard and so often it would almost bleed. It would be nice and raw by the time I entered on many occasions. She loved it; she was a real submissive. I would force her to suck my cock and then usually finish fucking her hard doggie style or deep-throating her. No foreplay, no post chitchat. I never really hung around afterwards, and in the end I just stopped going around there because I didn't have time. She did want more as in a relationship, but I just wasn't the guy for her. She never refused my crude advances and always accepted it when I wanted it. Even later on when she started another relationship and had a boyfriend. She always did what I wanted.

We cleaned the windows at her store all year and every time Layla and I would get up too a bit of mischief, usually with her blowing me or just jerking me off. I loved that. It was amazing. I would just come in and we'd do it at the back of the store in the changeroom. At work she would at times acted a bit nervous, saying we shouldn't, but she would always give in to me and let me have my way. I loved that I could come in and do the windows and then get jerked or sucked off every week by her and then go about my day. It was a great release early in the day and always put a smile on my face. The other girls who worked there eventually caught on and would smile when we came to do the windows and usually give us some space, but no one ever said anything, at least not to me.

A NAVAL ENGAGEMENT

JUNE

We were working in a bayside suburb, cleaning a couple of pubs' windows when the boss called saying he wanted us to do a quote when we were done. He wanted us to look at this navy military base about an hour out of town to quote the window cleaning. I was working with Billy, an experienced window cleaner from England originally, and neither of us was happy about doing it. Billy complained to the boss that we better get some bonus money for doing it. I was just upset as it meant I would be late finishing and that fucked with my sexual plans for the evening.

I had planned to catch up with Kim, as she had been getting a bit needy. I had stayed over and fucked her the night before and she wanted some more. Who was I to argue? We were going to get something to eat and then eat each other. Jeez, I loved fucking her. She was a sexual beast. She fucked me like no other woman. Mostly when I was with a woman I did the fucking, but with Kim when she decided she'd had enough of sucking my cock and wanted to climb on top, that's what she did. If she wanted to ride me like a cowgirl, then who was I to argue? She would slam herself onto me too whether on top, which was quite often. She loved it that way or doggie, when she would look back angrily and force her arse into my cock. I would grab her by the wrists while fucking her doggie and ride her like a pony, fucking her harder and harder. I loved fucking her and I love thinking about her now.

Anyhow, this quote we had to do meant we would be late, so I was pissed also. We grumbled about the boss all the way there. When we arrived, we had to wait at security to be picked up by our escort. I wasn't even thinking at the time that this would turn out the way it did but was I in for a surprise.

We were waiting in the security office—more fucking around, we grumbled—when I noticed a car pull up. Out got a woman who immediately snapped me to attention. She was older than me, mature looking and a real woman. She didn't mind showing it either. She had high heels and a woollen dress that showed her shapely figure and plenty of leg. I couldn't believe my luck. At least I was going to have a good perv, I thought. Sue introduced herself and signed us in officially with the security guys. Every guy in the office was interested in Sue. She was just a real woman who boiled your blood. As she spoke with security, I looked at Billy and he raised his eyebrows. Even he had noticed this woman's pure sexuality. She led us out of the office and said to follow her car. I watched her arse bounce as she walked in front of us, enjoying every wiggle. As she approached her car door and got in her car, I deliberately followed closely so that I could enjoy watching her take her seat. She looked up at me suspiciously and I didn't back down in making it obvious that I was enjoying the view. I smiled and said, "We'll follow you then, hey?"

Billy was laughing at me as I got in the van, and he commented on about how obvious I had made it. "What?" I said. "If I have to be down here, then I might as well have some fun." And she looked like fun. Also, with this job being so far away I was probably never going to see her again, so why not be obvious. This would improve my chances, I told Billy. He just laughed.

I was a lot more confident sexually at this point, especially with the last couple of months under my belt and I just felt like I was going to make it as obvious as possible with Sue. I decided as we followed her car that I would make it obvious that I wanted to fuck her. What the heck was the worst that would happen? I would probably never see her again anyway.

A little down the road she pulled up and got out and pointed to where we could park our van. I just grinned at her, checking her out and imagining her naked and me giving it to her. Boy, I was getting myself into a funk. I said to Billy, "I'm going to fuck this one." He laughed.

"First things first. Let's at least give her the quote," he said. We both laughed!

Sue led us both into her office, where she got us a map of the base and took a phone call while we waited. I just perved on her the whole time and the more I looked the more I liked. She ignored me the whole time in the office, but I didn't care. I was determined to have a go and interestingly all thoughts of any of my other girls had completely evaporated. I wasn't even thinking about where I had to go that night. When she got off her call, she explained which buildings on the map she wanted quoted and that we would have to come in her car so she could show us the buildings she needed prices for. I thought, *I would love to cum in her car or anywhere else with her around.* We were cool with that and like a gentleman I let her lead us out to her car, perving on that beautiful arse wiggling with every step she took. I jumped in the front seat beside her. I looked back at Billy, and I could see that he was enjoying my antics and he just shook his head. As she started the car, I adjusted myself in my shorts, stretching them down to cover my bulge, which was nice and obvious. I felt like she noticed. I was wearing my footy shorts as usual and I thought I could use this to my advantage, at least in making it obvious that I was a walking penis. When sitting in her front seat, she couldn't help but see my legs and how short these shorts were. It was difficult to keep my tackle from popping out, especially when I was aroused.

We drove around the base with Sue pointing out different buildings and asking the occasional question, which Billy answered mostly. I was just enjoying the view and imagining things. Like what colour panties she had on, what her vagina looked like, what it tasted like, and how I was going to get at it. I always really liked to think what a woman's vagina looked like when I met a new one. With the amount of oral sex I'd been delivering in the past few months, it had become a bit of a new obsession I had. I also loved Sue's smell. She had a beautiful intoxicating perfume. I imagined it was her pussy. Every five minutes or so I gave myself a little adjustment and a bit of a squeeze. Like I said I was going to have some fun. She didn't seem to notice and played it cool and professional, and we returned to her office after about what seemed twenty minutes. She thanked us for coming, which made me smile, and she smiled back at my smile, and I thought I saw her blush. With that she turned and walked back into her office. I can still see that arse and hot strut to this day. Also, that smell. I was spellbound.

As we got into the van, Billy laughed and said, "You are a shocker. Could you make it more obvious, playing with your cock every couple of minutes?"

I just laughed. "What the fuck?" As we started to drive off, I said, "Hold on just a minute. I'm going to ask her out."

He said, "Fuck that. I want to get home."

I just opened the door and said, "If I'm not back in five you can go without me." I jogged over to her building. My heart was racing and I slowed up and took a couple of deep breaths. *Jeez! I'm going to look like an idiot.* I always got really nervous when approaching a new woman. It was just the way I was, and I was actually shaking. It was that feeling of rejection, the unknown I guess, and anyway I had only just met her and had no right to be asking her out. But with Billy waiting impatiently I had to move fast, so in I went. As I got to the open door to her office I was like nervous. I took a deep breath and stuck my head around so that I could see her. She was sitting at her desk but looked up fast as I sort of startled her.

"Yes?" she said, looking at me inquisitively and obviously wondering what I wanted.

I stammered as I was not really prepared—if you ever could be for this sort of reckless approach—and my words came out nervously. "Umm, I'm just wondering if you'd like to go out for a drink sometime."

She just stared for a moment that felt like an awkward minute and then she laughed kind of cutely, like she was flattered and interested. It relaxed me and I thought, *Shit here we go.*

Just as soon as I had that thought, however, she said, "No. I couldn't. I'm married." Then she just stared at me, waiting for my response or waiting for me to just go. I was feeling awkward and now and wanted out of there. I stood right in the doorway, fully embarrassed. I guess I deserved it. Looking awkwardly at her, I noticed her look down to my crotch. It was good look too and she looked up at me, quickly blinking. I could see she was maybe interested. At least in some cock.

This relaxed me instantly and I smiled and said, "Okay, goodbye. I've got to go," and then sped to the van, and we headed home. We laughed on the way home about how I'd crashed and burned. But I had got her attention. Sue was married so couldn't do anything, but that look at my crotch said it all. It had been worth a shot, and I could tell she wanted cock. Whether she was getting it or not was a mystery, but her look at me was a tell. I was learning a lot about women, and I knew that a sexually active woman would enjoy a tussle with me.

I arrived at work the next day a little worse for wear as I'd been up late fucking Kim, and she always insisted I give her one in the morning before leaving. I was happy to oblige as I'd woken up to her alarm hard as a rock. I folded her in half, pushing her ankles back behind her ears, and pumped until I came deep inside her. Once done I got dressed without showering and headed to work. I loved the smell of my women on me after sex as their scent would revisit me throughout the day and make me smile. When I arrived, Billy started telling the guys about me and Sue. It gave everyone a bit of a laugh. "What the fuck, that's what we do," said Wayne. "We clean windows, drink beer, smoke weed, and chase pussy, not necessarily in that order." Everyone laughed.

A couple of days later the boss mentioned to Billy and me that the job at the Military base had come in. My ears pricked up immediately as we hadn't gone cheap and in fact we never did. It was a big job, a couple of weeks' work for a crew of four, we estimated, so it was going to be a task. It was also about an hour and a half from the office. The boss organised shifts of different guys to go down to share the load as was his way sometimes. After the first week he asked if anyone was willing to stay down there for the second week in an effort to get through the job quicker. Andrew, Simon, Peter, and I decided to go, and we had a hoot.

The boss put up the motel rooms and meals, and there was some nice bonus on offer. I thought it sounded like fun, and I had been down there about four different days already, and the driving sucked. We didn't see Sue much either. We mostly just arrived, signed in, and went to work, always wanting to get out of there as soon as we could. I was also feeling a bit embarrassed, awkward, and was happy not to bump into her. I did however remember that look she made at my cock, and I wondered. We had a mad time while down there, every night hitting the pub for a counter meal, plenty of beers, pool, and then back to the motel room for some cones. I was falling asleep wasted every night around midnight, but it was fun.

On the Thursday night there was a band playing at the pub and a bit of a crowd had rumbled in. We were all full of piss and cones already, and I was really starting to feel tired after such a big week of work and nonstop drinking and weed with these animals. I mean, Simon in particular was hard to keep up with. Once we got to the pub, the beers just flowed so quickly it was ridiculous. I was knocking down the beers and trying to keep up, and it was then that I noticed Sue. I looked over at a group of people and our eyes met. She smiled. It caught me by surprise and I kind of nodded, still feeling awkward but numb from all the substances. I kept looking over while drinking with the boys and noticed that she was continuing to look over at me. Fuck, she was hot too, great body, long hair, and just sexy. There was something easy about her as well. She was a bit of a bogan. I noticed this now or maybe it was just because I was drunk.

Anyhow, I drank up and decided to go over and say hello. The music was loud, but we managed to hear each other and have a little chat. She was out with friends on a girls' night. She introduced me to a couple of her friends. It was nice, and being late and drunk, I would have done any one of them. I also hadn't had sex since last Sunday night, so I was good to go. They were all pretty fuckable too, older than me, but I only saw that as a bonus, and I was just aroused in their presence. I was getting along with them and I'm sure I could have got with a couple of them by the way they looked at me and we interacted. I thought to behave myself, though, because of Sue. I don't know why. It was an awkward but stimulating exchange as I felt like maybe there was a chance with her. I just didn't know how to move it along. She was married after all, not that that would have stopped me. I was hot for her and loved her smell. The other guys noticed us and were soon over carrying on like idiots. I had to tell them that this was the client and we needed to behave, which was difficult to achieve as we were all hammered, and they just didn't really care. Simon introduced himself by saluting to all the ladies and saying, "All aboard." Simon, Andrew, and Peter were trying hard to get onto the ladies and get them to come back to our motel for cones and although I detected some interest from some of Sue's friends, we ended up parting ways and leaving them alone. We were just too damn wasted. Otherwise it might have turned into a wild night. Sue's friends were sexy, and I got the feeling under different circumstances we all could have got laid.

The next day was Friday and all of us were looking forward to getting the job finished and heading home as quickly as possible. We were all hungover as fuck and I was especially keen to get home and get into some pussy. I was horny after a week of no sex and thinking of Kasey and Kim. Also there was Layla. I was really looking forward to fucking her. I had a few to choose from now and I still hadn't called her. I couldn't wait to get back to it. I was thinking what I would do was head over to Kasey's work to say hello and try and get some in the stockroom and then head to Kim's and fuck her. Friday night was organised.

We were nearly completed around midday and Andrew, the senior man, suggested that I let Sue know that we were done. I said, "Okay, sounds like a plan." At least it gave me another look at this beautiful bogan. I drove over to her office in the van and went in. Sue was alone in her office, and she looked good. She was wearing a grey woollen dress that hugged her beautiful body and showed off all her assets. It had big white buttons at the front that went down to her waist and was that tight on her that it just screamed to be undone, I thought. I told her how beautiful she looked, and she thanked me, blushing. She really liked the compliment. I couldn't help myself. I let her know that we were nearly finished and would be going soon if there wasn't anything else.

She thanked me and we chatted briefly about the night before. She thought it was funny how wasted we were and that we had made quite an impression on her friends. Apparently, we had made the night a lot more fun. I was a bit embarrassed still in her presence. It was weird as it didn't really matter. I was about to leave when she suggested that she come out and make sure we had gotten every building. She didn't want us to miss anything and have to come back. At first, I thought that was fair enough and made sense, but as she got up and grabbed her handbag, I couldn't help the urge I had to get with her. She was sexy! She had these little black come-fuck-me boots on that just complemented the whole package. Fuck, I was horny for her.

She brushed past me as she walked out the door. Her office was quite small, and this was the first time we had touched. It sent a tingle through my body as it was a sample of her, and I really wanted more. I walked quietly to her car, feeling a sexual energy around her. I started wondering if the way she was dressed was a bit of a show for me as was the brushing past me as she had initiated it. Also, the night before she did look like she could be interested in me. She seemed interested and even jealous when I was getting along so well with her friends. We drove around the base past the buildings we had cleaned, mostly in silence, but occasionally she asked me if we'd got that and pointed to different buildings. I could feel a real tension and had to work at relaxing but the feel and sight of her so close was a tease, those beautiful legs in those dirty boots, her full hips and tiny waist, and of course those large breasts. Her smell as well was just intoxicating. I was dying to know what she tasted like. Her husband was sure a lucky man.

At this point I asked her what her perfume was, and I told her it was intoxicating. She shook her hair suggestively also was quite a turn on. At all these signals I was becoming so aroused but was also calm. We started driving down a smaller road with scrub on either side and no buildings. The sign had said Ammunition and Rifle Range. We got to some sheds, and she drove the car around the back of them and stopped. I was a little perplexed until I suddenly realised what was happening. It was like I had just arrived at a surprise party with everyone jumping out and screaming, "Surprise!"

I turned to look at her and ask what, but the passion just took over. We came together, locking lips, and we just started groping at each other. We kissed passionately and both were breathing heavily. As it turned out she had been getting herself into quite a dither also and needed a release. Wow! What a turn of events. I never saw this coming but wasn't going to let that stop me from getting into it. We kissed and kissed passionately. I unbuttoned a few of those big white disks to expose her breasts, big full things that they were. I slobbered away furiously, ripping at her lacy bra to try and get at them fully. She had to push me off so that she could remove it. Once out of the way, both breasts were fully exposed, and I dined on them. Grabbing them with both hands, I squeezed, kissed, licked, and sucked on them for ages. Occasionally I came up to kiss her neck and pash, but I just kept getting on her tits. Her pleasurable moans drove me on.

Sue was also returning fire and had released my bulging cock from my shorts with my help, of course. Going at it in her car was a bit of a challenge but we didn't let that stop us. I had slipped my cock out the side of my shorts and she was cranking it hard. It felt great after a week of no action, if a bit rough! She was giving me a good hard dry jerk while I slobbered on her glorious jugs. I also now had a hand between her legs, which she opened willingly, panties pulled aside. I was fingering her. I increased the penetration from one to two to three fingers, going hard. She was so wet. I smothered her tits, neck, and mouth with sexual passion and slobber at the same time. In not too long she climaxed with a big scream and shudder. I had to stop as it seemed too much for her. I was totally lost in all this. It was so natural. It was where I wanted to be.

We paused for a moment to look around and then she grabbed my cock, which was huge and red from her jerking, dribbling precum, and she went down on me, sucking furiously like she hadn't eaten in a long time. She was hot for it, and this was as dirty and spontaneous as any sex I'd had in a while. Even though I hadn't had any sex all week I still wasn't cuming. She sucked hard, wanting to get me there, but my cock was hard and resilient. After enjoying a good amount of head from her, she asked me to lay my seat back, which I did quickly. It was a great idea as we now had a little more room, and I lay right back, pulling my shorts off. My full erection slapped on my body. I could see it covered and dribbling precum and saliva from Sue. Man, I was horny, and I could see she was too as she looked at my cock and me eagerly.

A moment later she was on top of me as I helped her insert my cock in her and we began humping each other. She was trying to ride me like a cowgirl but couldn't sit straight up as the roof of the car made it cramped. We met each other's thrusts somehow as best we could. It was intense. She was bent over the top of me because of the lack of space. I just hung on to her arse, her big melons swung in my face, and I bit and sucked at them as we fucked. We really went at it for quite some time in this position, fucking each other hard and noisily until Sue climaxed again. I was still hard, and we took a short break. Sue slumped back in the driver's seat. I still hadn't cum but was itching to and was still fully erect. I got up and told Sue to lay back on my seat. We shuffled past each other to get into position, and I spread her legs as best I could and lifted her arse for the best available angle. I climbed on top and slid straight in all the way to the hilt. She gasped aloud and then said she wanted to make me cum and that it was my turn, and she was right. I started to get a rhythm going, pumping furiously as I was as horny as fuck, and I hadn't cum all week. I drove it in and out of her like a madman so hard and fast I could notice the car rocking violently about. She was moaning loudly and screaming with pleasure, and this really made me go for it hard. I pumped her as hard as I could, given the cramped confines of her front seat, and within a minute I was bursting deep inside of her. I really slammed into her hard. It was a huge orgasm and release of sperm. It was quite an eruption as I hadn't cum in a week and I really thrust it deep and hard as I finished. I was so into it and when done, I just collapsed on top of her, breathing heavily, matching her, my cock still hard resting inside her. After a minute I took a quick look around as best I could as the windows had fogged right up, making it difficult to see, but there was no one around. We smiled at each other and had another nice long kiss. I told her, "Now that was fucking grouse!" I slid my cock from her, and we both straightened ourselves up quickly, catching our breath.

We had to get out of the car to do it fully and Sue lit up a smoke. We just smiled and laughed as she finished her smoke and recovered. "You better get on your way, I suppose," she said.

As we drove back to her office, I said, "We must do that again." She agreed. I gave her a kiss and her tit a squeeze before I got out and she gave me a business card and smiled. "See you around," I said.

FROM THE JOURNAL

Today I fucked this woman in her car at a job at the naval base. She was the main cleaning supervisor and I had been hoping to have a go at her, but it took me totally by surprise. I never thought anything would happen after I had asked her out and she declined, telling me she was married. I guess she wasn't as married as she said. She drove me around the base, checking out our work, and then we ended up parking away behind some sheds and went at it. Amazing. I didn't see it coming until she was on me. It was like my own personal surprise party. Thanks, Sue. Looking forward to catching up soon.

FROM THEN ON

I went on to see Sue for a couple of years. We had a really nice relationship where I would just meet up with her when I wanted. I mean, I never treated her disrespectfully. She liked it this way and encouraged it. We had great sex together as she was separated from her husband, and she was hungry for sex still. I could turn up late at her house or meet her at the pub after work for dinner. She was just always very obliging. I ended up ruining the relationship with her by fucking one of her friends at a party. She caught us in the act in a bathroom. It broke her heart and mine to a bit.

METER READER

JULY

Shay, my surprise meter reader

It was July and the weather was cold in my city. It was a quieter time of year for the business and a few of the guys usually took holidays this time of year and headed either up north or overseas. Because of this I had been working a bit on my own over the past couple of weeks and I was enjoying the freedom it gave me. It gave me the ability to make a lot more money. I was on my own and even though the business was a bit slower there was still plenty of bonus to be made from houses and other works. The real bonus, though, was the ability to get around to some of my girls and give them a good going over. I was able to get around to Kasey at the pub before it got too busy and had fucked her three times in the week. It was great. I did my shop runs and by the time I was done she'd be starting at the pub, so I'd sneak in and do her in the stockroom. I really enjoyed a midmorning suck and fuck, and Kasey didn't mind either. After this I would finish my day and either call on Layla as she'd get home around 4:30 p.m. or rock up at Kim's. Either way we'd get straight down to business, and both liked it and to be taken. Layla had given me head one morning when I did the shop run that week, so I skipped the morning fuck with Kasey and headed to Kim's that afternoon. It was just a merry-go-round of pussy and I controlled the schedule. Actually I was completely out of control. Being on my own so much just made me want to bounce from one fuck to the next. Because I had so many casual options, I just went full on. There were several days when I had three different women in one day. I would fuck Kasey, then Layla, then spend the night with Kim. I did this three days in a row before heading home one night to give my cock a rest. But sure enough the next day I was at it again and looking for more. It was this that led to a real dirty surprise encounter.

I was cleaning the outside windows on this house when I suddenly noticed this lady walking around the front yard looking at the ground like she had lost something. She looked like a gardener the way she was dressed but it turned out she was a meter reader. She was going door to door reading the water meters. I said, "Hello."

She looked up bright as the day and said, "Nice day, hey!" even though it was cold. She had a green beanie on her head a green long-sleeve top and a thick neck scarf. She also had glasses. I remember my first thought was that she was cute. I could tell that she was quite petite because there wasn't much of her, and her face was thin. She asked me if I knew where the meter was in this damn yard. I didn't know but offered to help. As we looked around, I immediately started checking her out, the dirty perv that I was, and I decided quite quickly that I'd give her one. She had these dark blue work trousers on, and they showed of her nice heart-shaped arse. When I noticed this, I thought. *You couldn't, could you?* She found the meter and squatted down to read it, showing off her beautiful arse even more fully as the pants tightened as she squatted. I stood behind her thinking. *How could I get this going?*

When she got up, she asked me, "Aren't you cold in those shorts?"

I was happy she had noticed and just fired back with, "Well you could warm me up."

She smiled and laughed but to my surprise then said, "Maybe when I'm done. I've got to keep going." I was totally surprised. It sounded like she was interested.

I pressed, "Are you sure? I've got a nice warm van. I could get you out of the cold for a while." She laughed again, smiling and giving me an inviting look as she headed off. I yelled out, "Well, what about after work?" She laughed again as she walked off and waved.

I was like, *Oh well, nearly.* It didn't matter anyway as I had already fucked Lyn that morning and I was planning on visiting Layla after work and then having Kasey come over. I always really liked a new adventure, though, especially of the casual sex kind, and I gave myself a squeeze. She was tough, I thought, and I watched her walk off out of sight, enjoying her moves.

She was sexy even in her work clothes. Wow, what about that a sexy meter reader. I finished the job about half an hour later and a light drizzle had settled in one of those cold wet days where the rain just doesn't stop. As I headed off down the street, I saw the flash of fluro green and recognised my meter reader and I pulled over.

It was getting very wet outside now and I suggested she hop in. "Come on in. I'll get you a coffee and you can warm up and dry off."

To my total surprise she jumped in eagerly and we headed to a takeaway nearby. I introduced myself. Her name was Shay. We both got a hot chocolate drink and had it in the van with the engine running and the heater going. The heater was very good in the van and in no time Shay was removing her beanie and scarf. She had long red hair and was attractive with a crooked little smile and mischief in her eyes. I liked her. You can imagine my thoughts were going straight to *Where am I going to fuck this one?* I was excited but trying to play it cool. After finishing the drink, I returned her to where I'd picked her up as she asked.

The rain was falling heavily now and I was telling her, "There's no way you can go out in this." We chatted for a moment more. It was hot in the van now and then I just decided to tell her how pretty she was and in fact I thought she was hot.

She liked the compliment and replied with "You just want to get in my pants."

I said, "Yeah but you're beautiful." I leant forward, and with that we both just started kissing and groping. We had a nice long tongue bath. I was giving her a good feel, grabbing her arse and tits gently as we had only just met. She wasn't wasting anytime however and had been giving my cock a good stroke through my shorts and had even manoeuvred it out with a little wriggling from me. She was jerking me vigorously. When we took a breath, it was steaming hot in the van so I turned off the engine so the heater would stop. While doing that she had gone down on me and was enjoying my cock. She was good too and gave it a nice suck until I felt like I could cum but wouldn't in the seated position. It was just too cramped. I suggested we get in the back of the van, and she agreed. She was keen and I wasn't going to stop it. The back of the van was disgusting, with dirty rags, window cleaning gear, buckets, step ladder, etc. With a quick bit of rearranging, it was tight, but it was more room than we had in the front, and we went at it.

Both of us kneeling, I took off her top and to my surprise revealed an elaborate tattoo that trailed between her tits and down to her tummy and out of sight. "Nice," I said, admiring the tattoo. I sucked on her tits, and she moaned with pleasure. It was hard on my knees, so I laid down some window cleaning rags, but it was worth the pain I thought as I pushed on. After a good suck on her tits and the occasional look at this tattoo I turned her around as she undid her pants. My cock was standing up hard and ready and she was admiring it, eagerly wanting it. I helped her pull off her pants, revealing her cherry arse and another tattoo on her lower back. It wrapped around to the front one; she really was a dirty girl. I was going to give it to her hard as I was really turned on.

She got on all fours with her head in the corner looking back towards me, staring at my cock as I entered her, and I slid in with ease. She was wet and wanting. She had a nice tight body. She was about ten years older than me, and she loved to fuck. I gave her a good solid rogering. It took me quite a while to come and I ended up pulling out a couple of times for her to suck and jerk me, which she did willingly and hard. She really gave it a good thrashing too. I've never seen my cock get so big! She pulled it that hard. She dragged the blood into it. She made a lot of noise too especially when I was fucking her. Towards the end she insisted that I fuck her in her arse. She spat on her hand and lubed it up with her juices and fingers. It opened nicely. I spat on it myself and was happy to oblige and pushed it in slowly at first as it took a bit but then continued fucking her until I burst in her arse, so much cum. She really squealed loudly when I took her in the arse almost like she was in pain, but I could tell she loved it. I watched my cum dribble out of her hole as she lay whimpering pleasurably, breathing heavily, and I sat back and caught my breath, admiring her arse.

A moment later she was getting herself dressed as was I, as this was not the most comfortable of environments and we also both had work to do. She really was a dirty girl and it had been a great surprise fuck. As she was leaving, I pressed her for her phone number. She declined giving me her number but said she would take mine. If I wanted to get together with her again, then it was her that would give me a call. I knew this meant that she had a boyfriend or other and

I was happy with that. I did insist that we get together again in maybe some more comfortable location or if she just liked to fuck in the van, I would be happy to oblige. She thanked me for the good fuck, saying it was hard to find sometimes, especially from a hot guy but that I had been a pleasant surprise. As she left, I told her, "Oh, Shay! You made my day."

FROM THE JOURNAL

Today I picked up the meter reader and fucked her in the back of the work van. We had started chatting while I was cleaning a house and she came by reading the meters. We met up not long after and she joined me for a hot chocolate in the van to get out of the rain. We just got along really well really quickly. She was a horny little thing. With the weather as it was, we decided to fuck. It was an amazing fuck.

FROM THEN ON

I met up with Shay on and off for a couple of years. She was a bikie mole as it turned out. She hung out with a certain club and we had to be careful fucking, she warned me. She always called me, and I usually made myself available. She was a great fuck to a real dirty mole, and I always enjoyed our encounters. We usually met up for a drink—coffee, tea, or beer—and went to a cheap motel or did it in the van.

A DIRTY BUILDERS CLEAN

AUGUST

Billy and I were working together and after the shop run and a block of flats, we had a builder's clean to do. It was turning into a long day. The money would be good, so we weren't complaining. When we arrived, we both went inside as this is how we usually did jobs: inside first, then outside. The house was a renovated terrace house along the beach. It was a two-story terrace with some big and tricky moves for us and a lot of paint and builder's crap, so it would take some time. It had about a dozen rooms over the two levels and with the builder finished all that remained was for us and the general cleaners to finish it off and make it shine.

The general cleaners are where my fun began. We started upstairs and it didn't take me long to notice this tidy little piece working with the cleaners. She was older than me, mature-looking, and as sexy as could be for a girl in grey tights and a dirty white singlet. She was all tits and arse. Her outfit was snug on her and I was having a good look. She was moving around busily, ignoring us, but every time she walked by, I had to stop and watch as she just wobbled about the place in all the right ways. All I could think of was what a great set of tits and arse she had and that I was going to have a go at this if I got the chance. She was working with about half a dozen other cleaners, but none caught the attention like her. Ugly older women mostly.

Billy and I worked in different directions moving from room to room, so I was alone mostly. I thought, *Well, this might give me a chance to chat her up without anyone noticing.* I always found that sort of thing difficult in a crowded setting, small talk, etc. I moved into the upstairs kitchen, where a few of the cleaners were working, and we started to chat. My girl wasn't in there, but it didn't matter as I would bump into her eventually. While talking with the cleaners in the kitchen and listening to them bemoaning their existence as cleaners and how shitfull their pay was, my girl came wobbling and bouncing in. She grabbed some rags out of a bucket in the corner of the room, bending beautifully for me to enjoy. She moved fast, turning back out, never even giving me so much as a glance. As I looked back to my work, I noticed one of the older women cleaners had read my mind. She smiled and winked. I nodded in return as if we were both acknowledging her beauty and my dirty thoughts. At that point one of the ladies asked, "So how much do you guys make cleaning windows?"

I paused for a moment and then I just told them, "Well, it depends how much we make." They were curious and so I told them. "Well, for example, we get a percentage of the value of the job."

Pressing me further and now really interested, one of them said, "How much of a percentage?"

"We get a third each."

Well, I knew what was coming next and so I just let the cat out of the bag. After all these poor cleaners were making shit money probably, and they should know what was out there for them if they wanted to strive for something better. I told them that we were getting paid $400 for the window cleaning. With that I heard a scream from the other room. "What!"

Well, I had finally got her attention. She came bouncing in, working out the calculations. We were going to be making over $100 dollars each. She said, "Is that for real?"

"Yeah, that's right," I said, all calm and collected, enjoying her eye contact. She and the others were dumbfounded.

One of them even said, "But you have nearly finished the inside."

"Yeah, we'll finish this in a couple of hours." They were just in shock. Not only at how much we were personally making but how little time it was going to take. On top of that we were charging more than them, and they had six workers there for a couple of days. Well, I had tits-and-arse's attention now, as before this she hadn't even looked at me. Now she was interested. Who would have thought the high-earning lifestyle of a window cleaner would catch me the attention of a gorgeous woman. It certainly surprised me. I moved to the next room. Bob was on the ground floor by now, and tits-and-arse followed me in. She wasn't going anywhere either, which suited me fine. More time to perv, more time to work on her. While cleaning the window, she kept asking me questions, quizzing me, calculating, trying to work out how she could get into this sort of income.

I understood we were on a pretty good wicket. You could make some good money window cleaning and we did, and I knew it. She started to ask me if I would teach her how to do it. Interestingly her voice got quiet, and she even whispered to me that she didn't want her boss to know that she was interested in another job, or she might not have one at all. I told her, "Sure, I could teach you. It really isn't that hard." I was really enjoying her attention and I was getting an excellent eyeful as well. I suddenly had this position of power over her. It was nice. She was cleaning paint off the floor with chemicals and a small scraper. She had rubber gloves on and alternated between squatting and being on all fours. It really was a spectacular sight. Her outfit was so tight she was almost falling out of it while standing, let alone when she squatted or got on all fours.

I could see these pale blue panties through her dusty tights as she squatted and bent over, and her bra was clearly visible from under the way-too-tight, dirty white singlet. She had an excellent rack, big and bursting out of the singlet, and an arse I could paddle all day. She also had a beautiful VW bonnet on display out front that I kept perving at any chance I got. I really liked the look of her cunt in those tights. It was a sight. At that point I noticed her look at my crotch. She'd finally noticed my cock in the footy shorts. They always worked. She looked away quickly, but it was an obvious tell and I was going to use my power over her for both our benefits. I asked her quietly, "How badly you would like to learn how to window clean?" She was keen and would love to earn some real money. I was thinking, *Don't worry, you could earn some real money looking like you do.*

She asked, "How could I learn? Could you teach me?"

I told her that even though it was easy there was still a little bit to it, and it would take some time. I was just keen to bite on those big tits and put it into her. We were both working while talking. She was scrubbing at the floor, and I alternated between starring at her tits swinging back and forth and her perfect arse. I imagined her arsehole and vagina as I quite often do with a new woman. Wondering what they would be like. Will it be trimmed, bushy or bald? Will her arsehole be tight or loose? How will she smell? These are the questions that circled my mind as I perved on her beautiful arse. As I finished the window and had to head out, she sat back against the wall, her legs spread knees up, big tits and cleavage on display. She looked a sight staring up at me. I could feel my cock stir and I deliberately pushed it forward towards her. I had a great view of this fully voluptuous woman with dark hair in a ponytail. I looked down on her. I looked down through her tits to her twat, both bulging in her tights. I imagined her vagina was moist and sweet and needing a sucking. Like a juicy ripe orange, I would love to have a go at that. As she looked up at me, she said, "I'll do anything if you can get me out of this crap."

I was so turned on at this point I replied suggestively, "Anything?"

She nodded smiling sexily and whispered, "Anything." She could tell I was into her and was now playing at something and I was hoping we were thinking the same thing. If it wasn't for the other cleaners, I could have pulled my cock out right there and placed it in her dirty mouth and I reckon she would have taken it.

I told her, "Look, I'm heading out the back in a little bit. If you want to come out there, I'll show you how it's done or at least I can get you started." She smiled and agreed, and I headed downstairs to see where Billy was at. When I saw Billy, I told him about this woman's tits and arse. Billy laughed and seemed a bit jealous as he had also noticed her ample assets. I told him, "She'll be an easy lay. She wants to learn how to clean windows and I'm going to give her some lessons." Wink wink nudge nudge!

He shook his head and said, "Just don't fuck around too much. I want to get outta here." Billy was always about getting jobs done as fast as possible. It was fair enough as we needed to get the job done, but fuckin' hell this chick was hot and I was going to have a go if I got the chance.

I headed out to the backyard of the house and further to a garage that was located right at the back. It opened out onto a laneway out the back and had several windows in it that needed a scrape and a clean as part of the builder's clean. There were a couple of old dusty cars in the garage, and I was just about to get started when she came bouncing out and into the garage. She introduced herself as Tina, extending her hand to me, which I shook gently. I enjoyed her soft touch.

"I'm Dick."

So she was all eager to learn and said, "Well, I have to be quick though because I'm meant to be working inside."

I told her, "I'll just show you the beginning basics but then we will have to catch up at another time and do some more if you really want to get it." I was thinking this will be the best way to get with this babe. She agreed with this, and we began. I told Tina to watch what I was doing. As I started to clean the first window, I noticed my own nervous anticipation being near her had made me quite breathless with anticipation as she was so sexy. I knew this feeling well as I always felt this way when around an attractive woman I wanted to fuck. I gave the first window a good clean as this would give us a good base for Tina to start learning on. I explained the process I was following while I cleaned the window as it was a similar process every time. I now dipped the dolly into my bucket and rang it out and handed it to Tina. I told her to wet the window up like I had done. She wet the window up awkwardly as to be expected for her first time and then I moved in and showed her how to use the squeegee. She was very excited to be learning this. It was kind of cute and with every movement I couldn't help myself enjoying her gorgeous assets bouncing around. It made me smile and also excited with anticipation. We kept going over the process and repeating and as expected she couldn't do it very well. She just needed to keep practicing the same as anybody new to anything. "The more you do it, the better you get," I said.

We were quite secluded in the garage, and I was really enjoying being so close and alone with this beauty. As she was struggling and getting a little bit frustrated, saying she can't do it, she needed help, I moved in to assist. I moved to stand behind her, putting my hand on hers, and helped to guide her actions with the dolly and then the squeegee. As it turned out it was the perfect move. With the car in the garage next to the window we were practicing on, it meant that we were very close together and as we moved, her arse started to brush against my cock. When it first happened, I immediately felt some movement stiffening as I was already a little bit chubby and then Tina just kept backing up on it. With every practice, she kept pressing her arse back and so I obliged and pressed forward. We were still going through the motions of learning to clean a window, but in the end, it just became so obvious that I was rock hard in my shorts that she turned, smiling, and asked, "What do we do with that?" looking cheekily down at my predicament.

I smiled back and grabbed her hips, pulling her back into me and grinding my firmness on her soft sexy arse. She met my force by arching her back, lifting on her toes so she could enjoy my stiffness more fully. She cooed as I moaned, and I took a quick look to see if we were out of sight. We kept grinding at each other for about a minute, making my cock so hard I was really flustered. I couldn't believe my luck. I squeezed her tits hard while pulling her against me. Without any talk Tina turned around, placing the squeegee down, and helped me release my cock from my shorts. Her hands were cold on my cock as she gave it a jerk while I groped her breasts. With my cock standing firm, she squatted straight down and gave it a lick and then a quick suck. *How good is this?* I was thinking when just as quickly as she started, she stopped.

She stood up and said, "We can't do this here."

I said, "Yes, we can. It won't take you long if you keep sucking like that." I was going to cum quite quickly as all the prelude had really turned me on.

She was looking around and out towards the house, saying, "Someone will find out and I'll lose my job for sure."

There was nobody there and I just grabbed her and said, "C'mon, I don't give a fuck. Just suck it." I pushed her down towards my cock. I was leaning back on the dusty car bare bottom, and she just sucked away quite furiously. It was a beautiful feeling being sucked and jerked by Tina in the dusty old garage. I couldn't believe my luck. I reckon it was about a minute later and I was blowing my load down her throat, holding her tightly against my body as I enjoyed my climax. She gagged at the end and gasped for air, even coughing. I'd really messed her up as there was semen running down her chin and across her face. I handed her a rag and she cleaned herself up quickly. Pulling up my shorts and packing myself away, breathing quite heavily myself, I needed a break and I just stood there leaning back on the car until my breathing returned to normal. Tina looked at me as if to say she couldn't believe I'd made her do that and then glanced nervously back to the house to see if anyone had noticed. No one could see unless they were in the garage. I told her, "That was great, thanks."

She looked at me, her mouth open almost in shock at what we'd just done. "I don't even know you," she said accusingly. "You are bad. I can't believe you made me do that." She walked quickly out of the garage and back to the house. I thought it was fantastic.

I then went back out to the van and got a ladder so that I could complete the high windows at the rear of the house. I listened as I walked through the house to see if there was any commotion. There wasn't. Tina wasn't telling anyone. I noticed Tina a couple of times through the windows, and she would just pause and look at me with this shocked look, mouth open. It just got me hornier for her. When we were finally done and packed up, I told Billy I was just going in to drop off a card. He laughed. I quickly found Tina cleaning a toilet. She was on all fours, so I enjoyed her arse momentarily before announcing myself.

"Tina," I said, "if you would like me to give you any more pointers or window cleaning training, give me a call." I handed her my phone number. She looked up at me with the same open mouth, half shocked, half horny, without saying anything. She was so hot to be fucked, I could tell. She was horny as hell. Sucking my cock can do that to a woman. I asked for her number quietly as I wasn't sure whether she would call me after what had just happened. She seemed kind of angry. I wasn't sure whether she was mad at me or herself, but I certainly wanted some more. She told me quietly that she would call me that night and sort of shooed me out. That was good enough for me, so I was on my way quite happy with myself. I really loved an impromptu head job, and I was feeling great and relaxed as we returned to the office. I really couldn't believe I'd pulled that one off. But as I was beginning to realise a lot of women want sex and they don't mind a stranger even if it is the window cleaner. When I saw the boss, I got the details of the builder we did the job for. I thought that I could find Tina through them perhaps if I didn't hear from her. Tina was sexy, and I wanted to have another go at her. The sooner the better I thought. She needed to be fucked and sucked.

On leaving the office I headed to Layla's house only to find that her flatmate was home. This interrupted our usual routine briefly, but I didn't really care and after some small talk I took Layla to her bedroom and fucked her. While fucking her all I could think of was Tina and I gave it to Layla while I imagined it was Tina. They were similar, I thought, all tits and arse. I fucked Layla with a real furiosity that time, doggie style until I busted inside her.

FROM THE JOURNAL

Today I received the most glorious surprise head job in the garage by this sexy lady Tina. She was working with a team of cleaners at this renovated terrace house. When we arrived, I noticed her straight away. She was sexy with great tits and arse. She was interested in learning how to window clean, so I gave her a lesson out in the garage. We were alone in there and one thing led to another and before I knew it, she had given me the best head job I'd had in a while. This was a great day.

FROM THEN ON

I gave Tina about half a dozen window cleaning lessons as she really did want to learn and make more money. Every time we met at her flat, and after the lesson, I would fuck her. She had a boyfriend so I would only meet up with her when she called it and she was sure he wouldn't be around. I really enjoyed fucking her. I just did whatever I liked to her, and she copped it and loved it. She really was a dirty girl and loved the casual sex with me. I loved the kind of exchange for the training was that I got to give it to her.

"I'M A MARRIED WOMAN"

SEPTEMBER

I was working on my own this day and I had a quote and do in the 'burbs. The word was that it was a large two-story house, so after I'd done a small shop run, it was to the house and then home according to the boss. I'd been busy sexually and was quite happy with my roster. I had so many options for sex. It was just a great time to be alive.

Shops were an easy job and so were houses, so it was quite a stressless existence. I remember having thoughts about what I was going to be doing on this day and that it was finals time. Our club had a big game that weekend. I was thinking about that and that I would need to be sensible this week and not overdo it, and by that I meant wear myself out sexually or get on the grog. There would be plenty of time for that after the game. I used to wonder whether having sex before a game was good or bad. I'd even tried to survey it by doing it and not doing it. I couldn't really tell. All I really could tell was that I liked having sex anytime and all the time and that I liked playing footy. Survey complete, I thought. I did decide not to have late nights that week as I wanted to be rested and ready to go. In saying this, it was funny that some of my best football performances were after I had partied all night long, so you figure it out.

I arrived at the house around 10:00 a.m. and was greeted by this Greek mumma and a couple of kids. She was babysitting. I told her that I would give her the price, but I needed to have a look around first. When I came back to the front door, I was trying to tell her the price, but she didn't understand me. She headed back inside and got on the phone. I could hear speaking in Greek but was none the wiser. She eventually communicated to me to just wait ten minutes. Someone was coming home. I thought, *Okay, crazy lady.* I was a little bit pissed, as us window cleaners don't like waiting around. It's in and out as quickly as possible. I was waiting in the van and this nice Mercedes rolled up with what looked like a bit of a blonde bombshell driving, pulling into the driveway. I got out and headed back to the front door. As I came through the gate, out of the Mercedes hopped this absolute hottie. She greeted me with a big hello. Her name was Kerri.

"Wow!" I say. "I'm Dick and I'll be your window cleaner." It was a bit corny, but she smiled. This woman was hot and glamorous. She was done up to the nines as well, a real trophy wife. Her hair was long and wavy blonde, she had nice stylish clothes, tight jeans and heels, and long nails. I noticed straightaway, she was well put together and just had to come and get me and climb on board. I was a bit flabbergasted as I informed her of the price going cheaper than I usually would have. I was such a fool I went cheaper because I had reactively decided that I didn't want to put her off with a high price. She accepted so quickly even saying, "Why, that's very reasonable."

Damn it! I told her I'd get my gear and get started and I headed towards the car. Just as I got to the gate, I turned around quickly and said, "Oh, do you want your screens cleaned as well?"

Kerri looked at me a bit startled and replied, "Oh, of course." I fumbled out that it would be another $70, to which she just said okay.

I got my gear together and all I could think about was, *Wow, Kerri. I wonder if she's kinky?* I wasn't thinking about footy finals anymore. When I got to the front door Kerri met me and asked, "Where are you going to start?"

I told her I'll start upstairs, which was the usual procedure, and she said, "Okay, follow me."

I was happy with this because even though I could have worked this out myself, for some reason she wanted to show me the way. As I followed, I just enjoyed the view. I saw the old mumma looking at me suspiciously, to which I thought, *To rights I'm having a look.* As we headed up the stairs Kerri's arse was right in front of my face, wiggling sexily as she took each step and revealing a beautiful gap of daylight between her legs, which is one of the signs of a perfect arse. I couldn't believe this woman would not realise that I'd be checking her out. She was so hot but she hadn't noticed yet or so it seemed. After showing me the upstairs and apologising for some things, she got me to move a mirror that she said was heavy.

As I moved it, she said, "It's probably not heavy for someone strong like you." With that she asked me if I would like a drink.

I said, "For sure, anything." She then left me to it. She had actually put on quite a show prancing around, bending over to pick things up, huffing and puffing. It wasn't strange I'd been here before these lonely housewives. I could tell that she was enjoying having me around her. She was kind of flirting. Wow, she was flirting with me. Oh, I liked this as she was a real stunner, a mature woman but sexy as buggery, and I reckon she would like a bit of buggery.

As I cleaned the windows, I was thinking, *I bet she's not getting everything she needs sexually.* I could tell it was an amazing feeling and insight I had. I could really tell. I decided with this thought to see where this would go with a bit of encouragement from me, sort of like an experiment. What did I have to lose?

A moment later Kerri was back upstairs, inviting me down to have a drink and some cake. I followed her again as closely as I can get. I was thinking I might try to accidently bump into her, get to touch her and see what happened. I thought this would give me a bit of a clue as to what could potentially unfold. I chased her down the stairs and with my big feet trying to get close to her and I had a bit of a slip on the stairs at the bottom. I didn't even mean it but as it turned out it was the perfect result.

Kerri screamed, "Are you all right?" She turned quickly and grabbed my arms as I got myself back up. Once I was standing, she was all flabbergasted, stroking my arms and chest. I felt her nails and tingled. "Come and have a drink," she says, "and recover." It was a classic play by me even though I had actually slipped. It got her touching me and I got to feel her back. As she grabbed my arms, I got to feel hers also and even put a hand on her waist, pretending to thank her. Kerri had me sit and I enjoyed a cold can of Coke and cake. Mostly I just enjoyed watching her put on a show for me as I believed it was obvious. As usual I couldn't help but wonder what her pussy and arsehole were like. I would love to bury my face in that.

At this point I noticed that the old mumma was on to me. I was certain that she could tell I was having a right old perv so I was being as discreet as I could while still enjoying the show. Every now and then the old mumma would prattle something off in Greek that I couldn't understand, to which Kerri would reply also in Greek. I wondered if Mumma was alerting Kerri to my actions. I thanked Kerri and got back to work upstairs. I could hear the two of them downstairs having quite a screaming match and I continued to wonder whether this was because of my perving. I didn't care, however, because if I was going to have to work around this hot woman, I was going to enjoy the show.

As I finished the insides it became apparent the old mumma was heading off. Kerri also mentioned she was going to be taking her children to the pools as it was becoming quite a hot day. I cheekily said goodbye to the mumma as she left, and she just sort of snarled disapprovingly at me. It was funny, as I was having devilish thoughts about Kerri, and it was obvious. Kerri apologised to me for it, saying that her mother-in-law could be a bit grumpy.

I was on the outside now, and without the mumma there, I had decided to just come out and tell Kerri how beautiful she looked. I wasn't sure if I was going to be ever seeing her again anyway and I wanted to give her a nice big compliment. I also wanted to let her know I was interested and see where it went. When we next crossed paths at her kitchen window, I just said, "You are stunning."

She tilted her head as if she didn't hear me and immediately slid open the window, asking, "What?"

I repeated, "You are a really stunning woman." She loved it and thanked me. Fuck, I was horny for her, and I reckoned I could get her. The thoughts had me quite worked up. I continued cleaning windows and whenever we saw each other through the windows I noticed her looking at me. *Wow, I could get her.* It wouldn't take much but the kids, the job, she would have to make the move. I wondered if she knew I wanted her or could she sense it. I suspected she could as someone as sexual as Kerri like myself could sense it, I believed. I'd been in this position with customers before and I had to let her make the move. All I could do was be a little bit suggestive and leave the door open. It was a fun position to be in and I was enjoying the game of it. I really liked showing my interest in a new woman and getting the same flow back in return. It was a real turn on.

The house was big, and I still had a fair bit to do when Kerri asked if I would like another Coke. I said sure.

She said, "I'll bring it outside to you." She also said she was going to be heading off soon with the kids to the pool if that was all right.

I told her that was fine as I was on the outside and could just leave when finished. We exchanged some nice smiles and she returned with the Coke. She asked if I really found her stunning, to which I said, "Absolutely. You're smoking hot."

She loved it. I told her that her husband was a lucky man. She made a huff and headed back inside saying that she'd be back shortly. She wanted to get my opinion on something. Well, this was very interesting. She was loving my attention, and I could tell by her huff that hubby was dropping the ball. *There's an in here*, I thought. *It could be time for her to meet Mr Pane, Dick Pane!* I chuckled to myself. I had made it obvious I was into her and now I knew there was trouble in paradise. I got back to work as I had finished the Coke and she was taking her time. I didn't know what was coming.

I was up the ladder on the final upstairs window around the side of the house when Kerri called out, "Dick, what do you think of this?" She was standing just out of the laundry door, and I nearly fell off the ladder. She was standing there in a white bikini, and she was stunning. She was a perfect specimen. She really filled that bikini just right. Her tits were large and perfect in white, and the white bottoms just showed her off beautifully. I slid down the ladder like a sailor, mouth open, gaping at her beauty. She laughed shyly and said, "Well, what do you think? Can I go to the pools in this?"

I just said, "No, you can't go out in that."

"Why not?"

I quickly told her that if she went out like that, every man who saw her would follow her home. I meant it too. Kerri in that bikini, or probably any bikini, would cause traffic jams. I told her as much and just kept telling her how hot she was. "You are incredible! I would love to," I told her. OMG.

She was driving me crazy at this point and I had started to develop quite a swell. She looked at me invitingly, telling me she hadn't had much attention in a while. I told her to turn around and she did a twirl. Her arse looked spectacular. I moved closer, breathing heavy I stared down at her tits and asked, "Can I touch you?"

We were out the back laundry door alone. I pulled her towards me, pressing my bulge against her. She sighed and I could feel her give in to me. I tilted her head back and bit gently on her neck and squeezed her arse, pulling her cheeks apart.

She muttered breathlessly, "If you are quick and can keep a secret." With that she turned and headed inside with me hot on her tail. I was sweaty from working and just wanted to go animal on her. She headed upstairs saying, "We will have to be quick as I've promised the kids we're going to the pool."

I was going to be quick, but I really wanted to have a good chew on this beauty as well because she was stunning. Her kids were watching television downstairs and I gawked at her arse, licking my lips as we headed up the stairs. She turned at the top and we just came together pashing and groping anything we could get our hands on. I pulled her top aside and was feasting on her beautiful melons. She moaned intensely, breathing heavily as we rolled around on the carpet. She stopped me and led me to the bedroom, closing the door. "We'll have to be quick, and you must promise not to tell a soul."

I promised. We kissed hard and I squeezed her soft buttocks hard. She was panting heavily. I pushed her back onto the bed and began to go down on her, but she stopped me saying, "No, not there. You can't touch that. I'm married. You can't do that."

I was confused and stood for a moment, and she ripped down my shorts, releasing my growing erection. She started giving it a nice, good suck and complimented me on my cock like she hadn't had one in a while. It was like she was going to climax by giving me a head job she was enjoying it so much. While she sucked me, I fondling her tits, squeezing her nipples hard and then leaning forward to grab her arse. With her sucking away, I was going to cum in not too long with the way she was going but I wanted more. I wanted to fuck her. I pulled my cock away from her and laid her back on the bed. I went to climb aboard and enter her but again she stopped me, this time saying firmly, "No, I can't. I'm married."

I realised she didn't want me to touch her pussy. I was okay, but we were both like really turned on, so we had to release somehow. At that moment she rolled over and said, "Stick it in my ass. Just give it to me in my arse. I love it that way." It sounded good to me. I was busting to fuck her at this point. I was going to give it to her hard I was so worked up. She raised her arse high in the air, pressing her face down flat on the bed but looking back at me. I climbed excitedly behind her, spitting on her hole, and started to push it in. It was difficult to enter her, and she stopped me and rushed to her en suite. She returned with some oil, which she applied to my cock, giving it a good hard stroke for about thirty seconds while I played with her tits. She then pointed her arse toward me and applied oil liberally onto her arsehole, pushing a couple of fingers in to lube it up. It was quite a sight, and we began again with her pulling her cheeks wide apart this time. With my cock fully erect and aching, I pushed it right in. I quickly got a real rhythm going and in no time, she was climaxing loudly. Kerri was a real screamer and with her children downstairs it was a little over the top. She sounded like she was in pain, and I was even thinking the neighbours might hear. I continued to drive it in harder and harder and deeper and deeper, pounding away like a crazy beast, really fucking her hard and fast until I eventually pulled out and sprayed my load all over her arse and back. I just couldn't seem to cum inside her, and as time was of the essence it seemed the way to go. I blew a huge load. It was a great and wild fuck. We lay there recovering for a couple of minutes and then we both got back to business. I returned to window cleaning and Kerri, now dressed more fully, put her kids in the car. On leaving she handed me another Coke and made me promise not to tell a soul. I promised her my lips were sealed and enquired whether we could do that again. She said that she might book in another window clean sometime if I didn't tell a soul. I told her I'd look forward to it.

FROM THE JOURNAL

Today I fucked this absolute goddess, Kerri. I was working alone and doing her house when I noticed that she could be interested. I had been complimenting her on her beauty when she surprised me in a white bikini and then with an offer to have sex. She wouldn't let me fuck her pussy because she was married, so I fucked her in the arse. This was definitely one for the archives. She gave me a great suck and fuck.

FROM THEN ON

I cleaned Kerri's windows about half a dozen times after that as she used to tell me her husband didn't look after it. I could only ever fuck her anally. She loved my cock so much. She said she fantasised about me always. My boss was also impressed that she was so happy and a loyal customer and complementary of my work. We did it always in the middle of the day and I even met her husband on one occasion when I was leaving. It was fun while it lasted, but she ended it off for fear of being caught. I met up with Kerri some years later but that is another story.

MILK BAR MADNESS

OCTOBER MILK BAR MADNESS

I was working with Tony one day, and it was his usual Thursday morning shop run. I didn't work with Tony all that often, but the boss had put us together this day and that was fine with me. I really didn't care who I worked with or if I worked alone. It was all good to me as I got along with everyone in the company. We were enjoying a good laugh while getting through the shops on our run and at the end as usual around this time we were looking to break for something to eat. It was around 9:30 p.m., and Tony mentioned a particular milk bar he knew that had pretty good food, so we headed over to it.

When we got in the shop, there was this big Italian shopkeeper behind the counter. He took our orders. I was getting a chicken schnitzel sandwich and a can of Coke, and I can't remember what Tony was getting because I became distracted. As Tony was ordering, this beautiful sexy little piece came skipping out from the back of the shop. She was about my age, maybe a little younger, and cute. She had short dark hair and a gorgeous figure that you could see through the thin summer dress she was wearing. She had this tight apron on also, which really complimented her and showed off her nice tits. She grabbed some stuff from behind the counter and gave me a really sexy look and a wink. Wow, did she have my attention. I watched her return to the back of the shop out of sight. Just before she went out of sight, she turned and gave me another nice look. *Oh, this was great. I'm going to have to get to know this one.* I wondered for a moment whether the Italian was her father, so I moved discreetly to see if I could get a better view of where she went.

Got her! If I stood near the entry against the wall, I could see through the doorway that went out the back and see that she was working on our orders, putting our food together. As soon as I spied her, she also saw me and really turned it on at that point to my surprise. She kept looking at me while putting things together and winking. She also was bending over suggestively, arching her back while leaning against the counter. A couple of times she came back out to the main shop, and she was really putting on a show. This was fantastic as far as I was concerned as I had never experienced something quite like this. At some point Tony had even noticed it and came over and mentioned it to me. "Are you seeing this girl?" he said.

I tried to hush him up, but the Italian guy noticed and started yelling at what I assumed was his daughter.

Damn it! I tried to look like I hadn't noticed but it was a bit obvious, and I could see he wasn't happy. He yelled some more at her, but it didn't seem to stop her as she kept putting on a show for me. At this stage the crazy Italian was looking at me and then back at her yelling. It was becoming quite funny. Eventually she came out with our orders and the big Italian handed them to us. I smiled towards the girl, and he yelled at her to get out and then to us to go. It really was funny as at this point. I was walking backwards and having a last little perv and she was flicking up her tiny thin dress and apron she had on to give me a look at her knickers and arse. It was crazy. She didn't seem to care about the old man. It was like she was on heat or something and she had got my temperature up.

Tony and I sat in the van enjoying our food and having a good laugh about what had just happened. We had both never experienced anything quite like it. We decided that she was like a dog on heat, and she was after some cock, badly. I was also thinking about how I could take this further as even though Tony didn't seem interested, I definitely was. I told Tony as much and said I wanted to see where this would go. We would have to get on with our day so I decided I would go back inside quickly and get a donut or something else. I waited for some other people to go in and then I followed, hoping the old man wouldn't crack it when he saw me looking for the girl.

As soon as I entered the shop again, I saw the girl and she saw me straight away. Wow, she was sexy and really wanted it. I waited to be served and deliberately kept out of view of the big Italian by standing behind the other people in the shop. I snuck another look at my girl, and I noticed her motioning me with her hand and pointing over her head. At first I didn't get it but then it hit me like a bolt. She was telling me to come around the back of the shop. Oh, this was great. So I immediately turned and headed out of the shop. I didn't really need the donut after all. I did always enjoy a hot jam donut, but on this occasion, I had pussy on my mind. I ran to the van and told Tony that I'd be back in a second. I headed via the rear laneway to where I thought the milk bar was. I looked over the fences until I identified the milk bar and then I looked through the handhold in the timber gate. As I did this, I saw the girl come walking quickly out of the rear door. I watched her bending down to look through the hole until she came right up to the gate. She was cute.

I said, "Hey, you're a sexy devil," from the other side of the fence.

She opened the gate and kind of purred like a cat. "You don't know the half of it." She looked me up and down. She angled her arse in my direction, inviting me to touch, which I did. I ran my hand gently down her curved buttock, stroking it gently and then grabbing a handful and squeezing. She rolled her eyes, opening her mouth, and arched provocatively. Pulling away from my grip, she said, "I live upstairs above the shop."

I asked about the old guy. "What about your dad?"

She told me, "I can't talk now. I have to work." She told me to come by later and that she finished at three o'clock and that she lived up there alone. I was sputtering, "Are you sure? What about your dad?" I repeated. "He looks like he might kill me."

She replied, "Well, don't let him catch you then." She gave me a cheeky wink and, reaching forward, she ran her hand down my chest to my shorts. With a little lingering look she closed the gate. I bent down again and watched her walk back inside the shop, checking out her arse the whole way. Wow, this was going to be good. How easy was that? But what about the old man? I didn't want to get busted by him. He didn't look so happy at all. She didn't give two fucks and that was the least I was going to give her. I walked back to the van smiling about the rest of my day. I didn't even get her name. Ahh, who cared? There would be time for that later. I was just so excited that I was going to be having sex with a new girl. Jeez, I loved that. And so easy.

We whipped through the rest of our day, and I parted company with Tony back at the office. He wished me well, saying, "Don't let the old guy get you."

I laughed, but I must admit I was a bit worried about how I was going to go. It was about 3:30 in the arvo when I got to the shop, and I parked my car in a side street nearby. As I headed to her laneway, I decided to walk past the front of the shop first. I was nervous, not only from the excitement of having a new woman to fuck but also because of the potential danger of her old man, who clearly wasn't happy with us earlier in the day. I really didn't even know this girl. We had just had sex looks at each other and so this was quite crazy. When I got to the back of the shop, I stood back against the far fence in the laneway so that I could get a clear look at her unit. I was hoping that I would see her and get her attention because otherwise I was going to have to just go in and hope it all went well. I was really in a funk as I wanted this piece of ass. She had really turned me on being so hot for it herself. I paced around for a while, hoping I would see her, and then to my relief, she came out the door and stood on her landing shaking a tablecloth or something.

I jumped up and down like an idiot to get her attention and when she saw me, she laughed. She motioned me up but then also put her finger to her face to say be quiet. Fuck, great. Well, at least I had the go-ahead from her. With that I opened the gate slowly. It was unbolted. I looked at the shop's back door, which was closed, and up at her. She was smiling. I moved quickly from the gate to the stairwell and was up it in a flash. She was holding her door open, inviting me in, which I did quickly. She was laughing. "What are you so afraid of?"

"Your old man. He looks crazy."

Her place was quite cool. It had big windows all around, so the views were quite good, and it was just a cool pad. I introduced myself. Her name was Lilly. We chatted briefly, making small talk nervously, as this was just two people who just wanted to fuck each other. In no time at all we were at it on her couch, kissing vigorously and exploring each other. I was all over her, groping her arse, tits, and pussy. Lilly was quite cute and petite, and she was so horny. I was going to be able to do whatever I wanted. In no time at all I was licking her out and really giving her a good tongue bath until she started squealing so loudly, I had to stop. She looked at me as if to say, "Don't stop," but I was certain her father would hear so I stood up and released my cock from its tight confines.

As it sprang out, Lilly's eyes lit up with joy and she immediately began sucking and stroking it. It was like this was what she'd been waiting for all her life. As she worked my rod, I was thinking, *Well, she's done this before*, as she was just so damn good at it. I could feel myself cuming soon. I really wanted to pump it down her throat deep, but as I got close to climaxing, I pulled away and threw her face down onto the couch. Lilly responded by arching her back and presenting her arse high for me. With a light smack on her arse, I lined up my cock and drove it straight in. She moaned with delight and as I started to pump away, she got noisier and noisier. I was enjoying the ride but wanted her to be quiet as I was still nervous about her father downstairs.

I mean, I was sure that he might notice the ceiling shaking. I slowed my rhythm and told her to be quiet, but it didn't seem to work. I was really enjoying the fuck as well so stopping wasn't really an option at this point. I just wanted to cut loose and fuck her so hard she would be heard all over town. I had to improvise. With her head pushed hard into the couch I grabbed a cushion that was within reach and pressed it against her face. I couldn't hold the cushion in place and still pump her hot little arse, so I put my foot on the cushion and stood up. Now I could really pump her hard and with my foot on the cushion that was on her face. It muffled her screams. What a guy I was. I fucked her so hard and stood on her head. I got my rocks off. I held her tight as I came, really savouring my climax. As I pulled out, my cock still big and hard, she came up from the couch breathing heavily and started to kiss and suck it some more. She was really a nympho and wanted more. I mentioned, "Don't you need to be a little quieter?"

She just smiled and began to work my cock again. I laid back on the couch relaxing and catching my breath and letting her go to work. Who was I to stop her? It wasn't long before she was climbing on top and guiding my cock inside her. She bounced up and down like a maniac and I thrusted hard into her to meet her rhythm, squeezing her tits hard and occasionally pulling her down to kiss. We fucked like this for ages. She had multiple climaxes as we fucked and each time, I had to hold my hand over her mouth to muffle her screams. Eventually I flipped her over again and fucked her doggie until on climax I made her swallow my load. I deep-throated her and choked her hard. When done, she fell back on the couch gasping, and I was pretty spent myself. We both lay there recovering and eventually she put on a robe and offered me a cuppa. She put on the kettle. I put on my shorts and scanned the outside from her windows. We still hadn't even had a real conversation. I told her how sexy and hot she was and that I really enjoyed her. She told me I was the best fuck she'd ever had. As we sat enjoying a cuppa, I asked what would happen if her dad found out. She said defiantly she was eighteen and could do whatever she liked. I told her it might be best if he didn't find out. It was then Lilly told me that he shut the shop around 8:00 p.m. and that her parents lived at the back of the shop.

I asked, "Can they hear what goes on up here?" She smiled sexily and shrugged. She was crazy but a great fuck and I was going to get as much as I could.

It was around 5:30 p.m. and Lilly asked me if I would like some dinner. I could stay and eat and then we could fuck some more. Her mother always made her dinner, and she could bring it upstairs without her parents knowing she had company. It was a nice offer but having had a good time already, I was ready to beat it. I could return another time if she liked, I told her.

She didn't want me to go and insisted that if I give her another good fucking I could have her anytime I wanted. What was this, blackmail? I mean, it was a pretty good offer. She was sexy, cute, and a great little fuck machine and what a great pad I could access this anytime. So I agreed. I wasn't sure what would happen if I refused, as she was such a crazy little nympho. I also figured that now that we had got to know each other I would really give her a good one to go, especially after I had had a break and a hearty meal.

I was stinky from the day's work and asked if I could shower, which we did together. We worked each other over, washing each other thoroughly. I fingered her to climax once more, and she gave my cock a good clean, eventually finishing by fucking her standing up in the shower. Once we dried off and dressed, she went downstairs and in no time returned with dinner. It was some pasta dish and a piece of bread that was bloody delicious. It was dark now and I was paranoid people could see in as all her blinds were open. She seemed oblivious to the idea that when it got dark, and her lights were on, the whole outside world could see in. I suggested we draw the blinds closed, which she did. We sat on the couch after eating, making some small talk. She asked me if I had a girlfriend, to which I lied and I enquired about her. She told me she would like a boyfriend like me, someone who would fuck her well and regularly. She loved to be fucked hard and would do anything I wanted, she informed me. She really loved cock and wanted as much as she could get, she told me. She liked a man to dominate her and really tell her what he wanted and then she would do it.

At the time I didn't really understand the full meaning of what Lilly was saying, but with that we headed for her bed, and I ploughed into her for another hour. She put some music on, and I fucked her every way I could think of. I really fucked her hard as well. I licked her pussy and arse to climax several times and just kept fucking her until I eventually threw her down on the bed and jerked my cum like a sprinkler out over her exhausted body.

With that done it was time for me to go as it was getting late and I wanted to catch up with my mates. Lilly thanked me as I got dressed and asked me if I would come back tomorrow. I told her I usually went out with my mates on a Friday and weekends, but I could maybe come around later after I'd been out. She said, "Just come around anytime." She was hugging and caressing my body as I stood by the door ready to leave. I told her I would if I could and that I had a few things to do. She gave me her phone number but told me that her parents might answer but that was all right. She also said that if I wanted to come by late after I'd been out, that was okay also. "Just don't wake my parents," she said. So basically I could just rock up anytime and fuck her, with a caution. Exciting.

With that said I headed out her door and walked cockily down the stairs. I hadn't noticed in the shadows her old man. It was dark now and I couldn't see his face, but I could tell he wasn't happy. I looked back up the stairs for Lilly to offer some assistance, but she was nowhere to be seen. As I looked back towards her father, I could see he had a tennis racket and was challenging me to try and get past him. This was really a pickle I'd got myself into. I started to say that I was a friend of Lilly's when he lunged towards me, swinging the racket at my head. I reacted quickly, raising my arm to block the blow and running past him at the same time. He hit my arm hard, and it hurt, but I had no time to lick my wound. I got to the gate and instead of trying to open it, I just jumped up and over the fence as quickly as I could. "You crazy fucking cunt," I yelled as I ran down the alley. That was a close call and he had really hurt my arm with the blow but luckily no break. Ahh, what a day. I smiled as I headed home.

FROM THE JOURNAL

Today I met this little horn bag Lilly, who I fucked for hours in her flat above her parents' shop. She was such a horny little thing. She wanted it over and over and even after hours of sucking and fucking she was still up for more. Lilly invited me to fuck her anytime I wanted as she was always interested in sex and needed it all the time. Her words. Her old man tried to crack me over the head with a tennis racket as I was leaving. I was lucky I was too quick for him. He only hit my arm, and I got away by jumping the fence.

FROM THEN ON

I got together with Lilly lots, especially if there wasn't someone else I could fuck. Lilly also liked me to really dominate her and tell her what to do, which was something I had a lot of fun with over our time together. We had each other many times over the next two years and in many different and interesting ways. She would really do whatever I wanted and the more I realised this, the more I took advantage and really had some fun. We had sex in many different locations, and I could always rely on her to be into it. From a blowjob in the work van between jobs or my car to a hand job in the cinema, she would do it. We even went for it one day in the back of her shop while she was working when her parents were out. I had to keep stopping fingering and fucking her every time a customer came in. She was a lot of fun. She really enjoyed me fucking her anytime, anywhere. We ended badly as she found out I was rooting around as she was infatuated with me.

LADY'S DAY

NOVEMBER

Early November had a special day at the races called Lady's Day. It was part of a spring racing carnival in our city and was traditionally a bit of a lady's day at the races.

Of course, none of this meant anything to me. I was not interested in racing, horses, or the spring carnival, or at least I hadn't been up until this point. Well, all this changed on this day, and I can't remember missing a Lady's Day since.

I was working with Wayne and the boss had given us a usual day to start with a shop run followed by some flats and then, on returning to the office, he needed this big arse house cleaned in the inner city. The day was getting late and there were two crews working on it. I was on the outside. It had some high and tricky moves, and I was relieved when the high stuff was completed. While working on the ground out front, I noticed this limousine pull up over the road. I stopped to check it out as you didn't see this sort of thing every day. The driver got out and opened the door and these four women piled out, laughing and screaming. They were hammered. They were all dressed up really fancy, and it looked like they'd just come from a wedding or some kind of do. Several things that really caught my attention at the time were that they all looked nice. They also looked drunk i.e., easy, and I found myself squeezing my cock while watching them. They were all laughing and carrying on. At one point they all gave the driver a hug and a kiss, thanking him for looking after them. They even groped his arse. I saw it and thought, *This bloke could totally be in if he wanted it.*

I headed out to the street to get closer and then headed towards the van so that they would see me. I recognised that this was an opportunity that I shouldn't let pass. As I got to the van, they were taking photos with the driver of the limo, all of them in different combinations, flashing their legs all over this bloke. He really was "in like Flynn" if he wanted, but he didn't. I could tell. This looked like a job for Mr Pane, or as I liked to call myself, Dick Pane. That was exactly what they were going to get. Seeing this opportunity, I yelled across the road, "Hey, would you like me to take the photos so you all can get in it?"

With that they screamed, "Yeah! Woo hoo." I was like a saviour, and I noticed immediately that I was being perved on. This big-titted brunette handed me the camera with a little twinkle in her eye. I took a couple of shots all to various cat calls and whistles as they started to turn their attentions towards me. "Oooh, look at those shorts," "What a body," "Let's get some photos with him." Yep, next second the driver was taking photos this time, with me and these four sexy drunk strangers who were all done up in high heels and sexy as hell outfits. I had a good feel too, as did they while the photos were taken. This blonde hottie grabbed me on the stork and had a good feel. This was grouse. She even told the others, "Ooh, he's got a nice big cock." They all fell about laughing and screaming. They were hysterical. I managed to get from the driver that they had been at the races and that they were all mine now. He headed for the limo and drove off.

At this point the girls still a bit of a shambles, stumbling about. I offered to assist. "Could I help you lovely ladies get to your apartment?"

"Oh yeah," said the big-titted brunette, still looking at me with that twinkle in her eye. She needed some cock and so did the blonde. This was going well. One of the ladies, Sonia, as I later found out, grabbed the squeegee out of my belt and started enquiring about what I was doing and what I was going to do with her. Sonia was older than the other three but none less sexy. She had a nice tight slim body with long legs and a nice pair of tits with her cleavage nicely on display.

"Can you clean my windows?" she asked.

"I can clean all your windows," I replied cockily with a smile. They all loved the sexual innuendo and insisted that I come up to the apartment to have a drink and continue the day. After escorting them to their apartment, I told them I'd be right back as I had to let the guys know where I was. If I didn't, they would be wondering where I was. I headed out of the apartment block and ran across the road and was nearly hit by a car I didn't see. I was so excited. For a moment I thought about sharing what I was up to but then instinctively decided not to upset the situation as it looked like I was definitely in with a couple of these ladies and introducing another window cleaner just might fuck it up. What a guy I was, as usual always thinking of myself. I let Wayne know that I had to go and that I would make my own way home. He was suspicious and so I told him what was going on.

He was like, "Well, fuck that. I want to check this out for myself." I tried to put him off, but I couldn't. He wanted in and even though he was married as I reminded him, he laughed and said, "Well, we will see about that."

The apartment door opened and once inside I introduced Wayne and myself. The ladies seemed very lively still, and I could tell it wouldn't be long until we got down to business. There was a real sexual energy in the air, and I had already started thinking how I was going to bang all four of them. Sonia introduced herself with class, holding out her hand for me to kiss, informing me that it was her apartment and that if I was good, I could stay. We all laughed at this, and I could tell she wanted some. Wow, this was amazing as there was three of them. I was fucking for sure. Sonia then introduced my big-titted friend Paula, my cock squeezer blonde Holly, and Darla, a very sexy older redhead. All these women were sexy and had a real class about them except they were drunk. You could tell they were upper class.

Sonia got us both a cold crown lager and insisted we make ourselves at home. We sat on a large couch. Wayne looked at me excitedly, nodding with approval while he swigged his beer and started asking about the races. Sonia cosied up to Wayne and felt his muscular arms, saying he looked strong. Sonia had a short olive-coloured one-piece dress that showed her tits and crossed her legs beautifully. As she sat, both Wayne and I were enjoying them fully. It had been a hot day and the cool apartment was relaxing and the beers went down fast. As I finished mine, Sonia got up to get me another, revealing half her arse as her dress had slid up.

Paula sat beside me, pushing her big melons into my arm, which was starting to get me hard. Holly was behind, leaning over me, giggling. She said to Paula, "Go on, have a feel. He's got a good one." Next thing I know Paula and I are pashing and she's squeezing my cock. I return fire, releasing her huge tits from her pink-and-black polka-dot dress. I gave her melons a bit of love while she lay back moaning at the same time my hand was between her legs. She was as wet as an oyster. I looked up momentarily as I was wondering what the others were doing, and I was met with Holly's moist mouth. I sucked on her for a good time, feeling her tits and arse as I did.

While I was enjoying Holly, Paula released my cock, which was fully erect by now. She was sucking away. I helped Holly out of her clothes, revealing the most gorgeous body, big beautiful boobs, a great arse, and a beautiful full body tan. Just wow! I was standing now with Paula sucking my cock while she sat on the couch, and Holly and I were going for it, kissing and groping. I gave her tits a real go as they were spectacular. Biting, sucking, licking, I gave it all, all the while my cock was being vigorously sucked. I pulled my cock away from Paula and directed Holly to it. She didn't hesitate and took off where Paula was. I leaned down and spread Paula's legs wide and began to finger her quite vigorously, and she was loving it. I had to stop Holly as I was going to cum if I let her keep sucking.

I stopped fingering Paula and moved Holly onto her so I could fuck her doggie. The two of them started kissing and playing with each other's tits. It was grouse and quite erotic. I was so turned on and hard as a tent pole, so I started giving it to Holly from behind. As I was pumping, I could finally see what else was going on and it was a sight. Wayne was sitting back at the other end of the couch while Sonia was working his cock, deep-throating it as well, and he was just grinning at me and giving me a thumbs up. On the other side of the room Darla was sitting in a single seater with her legs spread fingering herself. It was a classic.

I fucked Holly harder, really giving it a good go, and then I heard Wayne grunt as he came. Sonia was a real lady and seemed to be licking it all up. I kept pumping away and noticed Sonia. She looked over at me as she straightened herself up and sat back on the couch. I pulled out of Holly, pushing her forward, and gave Paula a go. I pulled her legs right back and slammed into her hard. She squealed with pleasure. I was still so hard and didn't feel at all like cuming and I think it was because everyone was watching. After a minute or two on Paula I pulled out and let both Holly and Paula suck on my cock and balls. Within the next minute the two of them had me spraying my load on their faces, tits, and all over them.

Holly continued to pull and suck and I convulsed in pleasure. There was a bit of a cheer from Sonia as she seemed to approve of my performance. I collapsed on the couch, catching my breath, and noticed that Wayne was dressed and looking like he was ready to go. "You coming?" he asked. Sitting there naked, I looked at Holly and Paula kissing, and I shook my head.

"No way. I'll see you tomorrow." With that Wayne was up and out the door without even a thank you as I heard it shut. I looked over at Sonia, who was looking good, and I knew she needed some. I could tell she had gotten herself in the mood while sucking Wayne's cock. As I stood to head over to Sonia, Darla interrupted me and asked if I would take a shower.

"You guys stink," she said. "I could smell you the moment you walked in."

I was a bit stunned as I processed this request but then Sonia grabbed me by the hand and led me to the bathroom. "It's a good idea. Let's get you nice and clean as you have a lot of work to do still." Sonia joined me in the shower, and I chewed on her tits and washed her body as she did mine. She soaped up my body, really cleaning me fully and enjoying my cock and balls, and in no time I was ready for more.

We pashed in the shower, me groping her hard matching her as she jerked my cock. I ended up fingering her to a climax while pressing her to the wall, her back arched while I fingered both her snatch and her arsehole, really driving in hard. The noise she was making drove me on. Sonia made so much noise in fact that Darla came in to make sure she was all right. As we exited the shower, we grabbed towels and dried off. Darla cosied up to me, and we started to kiss.

My cock was hard again and pressing against her and she became like butter to my touch. I pushed her out of the en suite and back onto the bed. Pushing her legs apart, I began to kiss softly at first and then suck gently on her pussy. Darla was writhing with pleasure underneath my slobbering when I noticed Sonia slapping my arse. I was so hard and horny, having already cum once, and I knew I had some staying power under these conditions. I came up and drove my cock right into Darla with one big thrust to the hilt and started pumping away furiously.

Darla was screaming breathlessly as I was so horny and giving it to her so hard that it seemed like an assault. After some furious fucking, I decided to give her a break and turn my attention to the host Sonia. She was laying there smiling, and as I approached her, she turned her arse towards me and welcomed my cock. I now gave her a good fucking doggie style as I felt she deserved it. What an excellent host, I thought. As I pumped away, she climaxed again and again. I was so hard, so I just kept giving it to her as she was screaming with delight and asking for more. While we were going at it, Holly and Paula had come into the bedroom and joined us on the bed. Darla was standing getting undressed while Holly began to kiss my chest and suck on my nipples. Paula assumed the doggie position beside Sonia, and I took this queue to give Sonia a break and give some to Paula. Paula's arse was bigger and softer, and I really got to slapping against it with my hips as I thrust away, squeezing it hard as well. Things had turned into a full-on orgy by now, as Darla and Holly were going at each other and Sonia was pressing herself against me, sucking on my neck and squeezing my arse. I really was a plaything for these ladies, and I was loving every minute of it. With Sonia sucking on my neck, I started to cum and finished in Paula with some vigorous thrusts. I pushed Paula aside and lay down for a rest, catching my breath.

It was a big bed, a king-size, which I hadn't had a lot of time on before. I lay on my back with my head on the pillow, enjoying the scene. Four naked ladies and lucky me. Sonia cosied up to me on one side, playing with my cock as it recovered, while Paula leant over my face, big tits for me to feast on. I was hard again in no time and after Paula sucked on me for a bit, then Sonia saw my hard cock and straddled me and fucked me like a rodeo rider. At this point I really did become a plaything as each of them had a go while interchanging from my cock to my face. I was literally a man sandwich between the fluffiest white bread. I fucked them all, lying on my back as best I could while being smothered in their pussies. Licking, sucking, and fingering their holes all the while trying to breathe was an incredible achievement. After what must have been at least two goes each—I believe Sonia had three—I got to my knees and enjoyed being sucked until I came.

I was knacked after this and just lay back as did the ladies in a heap of bodies. They all started to nod off except for Sonia, who seemed keenly interested in what I was up to. I got up and wrapped a towel around me, making my way to the lounge to fetch my clothes. She offered me a drink, which I accepted, and I joined her in the kitchen. I was feeling incredible, and we chatted about the sex we had just had. She told me I was the best cock she'd had in quite a while, and I was welcome to visit again if I wanted. Perhaps next time she could have me all to herself. I was like, "For sure. That would be great." I felt like the biggest stud in the world. It was coming onto 8:00 p.m. and after having my fill, I said my goodbye. I briefly peeked back in the bedroom and said goodbye to the others, but they were out of it. Sonia was happy for me to go, I could tell, but she gave me her number and asked me to give her a call.

As I walked out onto the street, it suddenly dawned on me that I was on foot and had no car to get back to the office where my car was. I didn't care, though, as I had a feeling of total relaxation and invincibility like I had never experienced. As I walked down the road, my body, my balls, and my mind were totally at peace.

FROM THE JOURNAL

The most amazing opportunistic fuck fest of my life. A foursome of enormous magnitude.

Sonia, Paula, Holly, and Darla used me as a plaything like I've never been used by women before.

I lucked out on working across the road from where these four beauties got dropped off drunk and horny and with no one else around. I took my chance and I got to fuck them all multiple times. They had spent the day at the races and arrived at Sonia's house at the end of the day in a limo. I sleazed my way over, offering to take a group photo, and ended up having the biggest group sex of my life so far. Wayne my workmate also scored a head job and a deep throat one at that, as I saw him nearly choke Sonia while she gobbled it down. What a horn fest. I'm going to go back and have some more of Sonia and the others when I get the chance. Happy days.

FROM THEN ON

I visited Sonia many times and we enjoyed each other sexually. She was a high-class woman and I enjoyed sharing myself with her. She enjoyed my youthful energy and my obvious experience beyond my years. She loved the tongue and told me regularly that no man had done it like me and that I was truly special. Ha ha.

I also enjoyed her friends on occasions—Paula, Holly, and the beautiful Darla—but these stories can wait for another time. We enjoyed a few Lady's Days together.

Sonia also introduced me to a few other friends. One of them, Bree, had a kind of club happening, a sex club. No kidding. I'll tell more about this at another time.

THE HEAT IS ON

DECEMBER

It was late December, and the boss always had a Christmas party and put on the piss for the crew. This was held at a local pub that apparently hadn't paid their bill, so the boss was taking it out in kind. The boys were really getting stuck into the beers, and we were becoming rowdy. No one was going to interfere, however. With Simon, Andrew, Wayne, and Peter around, you would want to be committed. Even the bouncers kept their distance as we carried on like looneys. Everyone was telling stories about the clients, the year we had had, etc. Eventually it came out about me fucking the ladies on Lady's Day and several other encounters during the year. There were other stories from the other boys and even one about the boss pushing an orange up a stripper's arse and her squealing as the orange burst at one of the guys' final day send-offs. It was a good night and had been a hell of a year.

The night was getting late, and I was well pissed and thinking about what I'd do next. I had plenty of options and I wanted to get into someone and maybe even someone new. I was checking out the chicks in the pub but there was nothing really on offer, so I started to go down my list. Layla lived nearby but I was way later than I'd ever been there before, and I wondered how it would go. Her flatmate didn't like me, which put me off, but Layla was such a willing fuck it seemed an easy option. I could literally just knock on her door and start giving it to her, which was what I was thinking. Perhaps I might even fuck her right in front of the flatmate and get her involved as well. Okay, so that was that. My plans were formulated. Once we finished here, I would head over to Layla's and give her a good go and then make my way home. It seemed like a solid plan. As people started making noises about leaving, I noticed the boss head to the toilets, and I thought I would play a little prank. I had noticed a hose near the outside toilets and as he headed in the cubicle, I moved quickly to the hose. Throwing the hose over the door, I turned on the tap full bore. As I hastily headed back into the lounge, I said my goodbye and headed off to Layla's, giggling stupidly as I left. Fuck the boss. He could be a real prick and I was pissed anyway, so who cared.

As I pulled up outside Layla's, I was ready for sex. I really shouldn't have been driving. I was so pissed but not so drunk that I wasn't going to get some, and I loved fucking Layla. As I got to the door, I caught a glimpse of something through the window as it was dark outside, and their curtains were open, providing a good view of the inside. It was Layla's housemate, Lori. She was in her panties and bra and a nice setup it was as well. She hadn't noticed me, so I stopped and had a good perv. I looked around to make sure no one would notice me standing in the garden like a pervert. I continued to watch as she looked good. She had nice full tits and a shapely body and arse. The sight of her just got me hornier and I was already horny. I peeked through the window for quite a while until I could no longer because I just thought what a devo I was and that it wasn't okay. Sneakily, though, I thought maybe I could do them both. Why not? So I headed to the door and knocked. I saw the flatmate move with a start and then she was asking who was there. "It's Dick. Is Layla home?"

She was quick to inform me that she wasn't and that she was out with her boyfriend. This took me by surprise but in my drunken state I asked if she'd be long and could I possibly come in and wait. What the heck? I just wanted to fuck and the sight of Lori in her undies had me thinking. *You never know, maybe I could do her housemate.* She wasn't having any of it and told me to go. She didn't even open the door. She really didn't like me or the way I treated Layla, but who cared? Layla liked it. And what was this? Layla had a boyfriend? I was almost jealous and thought I would deal with her next time we caught up. And with that rejection I headed over to Kim's place, where I was greeted with open legs and a warm pussy. I gave her my best before crashing out, spent from alcohol and good living.

I awoke to Kim grinding against me and stroking my already hard boner. I quickly ploughed one into her as I was running late for work. She wasn't having me going until I'd given her one. Such was her way. I had a cracking headache too. I was hungover and dehydrated from the night before. Too much beer. Kim gave me a berocca (vitamin drink) to help me on my way and I sped off to work.

When I arrived, I was quick to notice I wasn't the only one rolling up late as everyone looked a little worse for wear and some of the guys weren't there yet. The boss had a go at me about the hose, which I quickly denied, and it seemed to throw him. I said it was Billy, and we all had a bit of a laugh about it, but he actually seemed quite pissed. I really knew he was when he gave me the job sheet. I was working on my own and all the way over the bridge in the west. What a shit gig of a day, but there was nothing to be done. The boss is the boss. At least its only window cleaning and I could recover throughout the day. Get it done and then head home for some rest.

I had a block of flats to do and then I had a house for some cleaner who owned a cleaning company. His name was Clint. I remember it well because I liked Clint Eastwood movies. It was a hot day and I sweated through what turned out to be a big block of flats but eventually had them done around midday. I was stuffed, so I stopped for some lunch and a Coke. Feeling better, I headed to the house with the aim of getting it done and heading for home. At least I was into a bonus and making some good money.

I met Clint at the house, which turned out to be his own house. He was a nice old fellow and said I was welcome to have a swim in the pool when I was done, given the heat of the day. It was bloody hot all right, nudging forty degrees. A real hot one. Clint wasn't hanging around either and just told me to shut the door and gate when I was done. His wife would be home later but if I was finished before that then, it was fine, and he headed on his way. Sweet. So I got stuck straight into it. The sooner I was done, the better. It was an easy house with big windows and I was done in about an hour. I shut the door, which locked the house, and then decided to have that swim as it was hot. As no one was around and having no bathers, I decided I would go in naked. I checked to see if any neighbours could see and decided it was fine. There was nothing like swimming naked. Freedom baby. I was jumping in and out, really enjoying my own nakedness and cooling off after working in the heat. The pool was so clear and cool and blue. It really was very relaxing, and after a short while, I decided to lay on the pavers for a while and relax. I was laying in the shade, but the pavers were hot still, and it really was relaxing lying there naked. I started to nod off. I probably was asleep for about ten or fifteen minutes, when I woke with a jolt. Wow, I really was tired, and it was just so relaxing lying naked on these pavers. It felt great also naked on the warm concrete, my tackle laying bare in the warm air. I got up and headed over to dive in the pool again to wake myself up and cool down, my cock swinging as I walked. I enjoyed the naked sensation of having my tackle out in the fresh air. It just felt so natural. I dived in the water and floated on my back for a couple of minutes. It was very relaxing. Suddenly I was startled by the sound of an opening door. I was not alone. Bloody hell, it scared me, and my first thought was *Shit, it's his wife, and I'm naked in the pool. Clint is going to think I'm a freak and this is awkward.*

To my surprise it wasn't either Clint or his wife. It was a younger girl, who was asking who the hell I was. I swam to the side of the pool to hide my situation and identified myself. It was all cool except for the fact that I was naked in a stranger's backyard. Marie was Clint's daughter, and she had a friend with her who had both decided to come home for a swim. They were university students, but given the disgusting hot day, she had decided to come home with a friend for a swim and a cool afternoon. She was perplexed at first to find me in the pool, but I quickly informed her who I was and what I was doing. I told her that Clint had said it was okay for me to have a swim.

After my awkward explanation she introduced herself and her friend Kylie and then informed me that they were going to be joining me as it was so hot. I told her that I would get going, feeling awkward and wondering how I was going to get out of the pool naked without them noticing. Marie said, "That's okay. You can stay. We're going to have a smoke and get high and relax if you want to join us."

This startled me and then what came next did as well. Marie then said, "Would you like a towel? I noticed how red your bottom is from laying on the hot pavers." Kylie was laughing and Marie was grinning. They had seen me naked already laying by the pool.

"That's right, we've been watching you from inside for a while."

I was embarrassed and worried that I'd be in trouble with Clint and my boss. Fuck, I was a cockup sometimes. I was flummoxed. I just wanted to get going and get my shorts on as quickly as possible, worried that Clint or his wife would be next. Marie didn't seem to care, though, and informed me that they would get their bathers on and be back in a minute. They both headed inside so I quickly took my chance and scurried out of the pool. I quickly put on my jocks and footy shorts and put on my bolle sunglasses as it was so hot and bright. I rinsed myself off under the outdoor shower and then was about to head off when they both returned in their bikinis. Wow! Now I was a little more interested. Marie had a camera and before I realised had taken a photo of me. *Shit, now there's evidence.* I was always thinking I was in trouble. The two of them looked sexy as in their little bikinis so I enjoyed the view momentarily as I prepared to leave. I told them, "I'll get out of your way then and leave you to it."

Marie said, "You don't have to go."

Kylie piped up as well. "Yeah, you should stay. We've already seen you naked so you might as well stay." They both laughed. At that point I was thought, *Okay, why not, what the fuck. Let's see where this goes. They seem a little interested.* I could always head off at any time if I needed and these two were pretty hot. In my experience also, once you had a woman down to a bikini there wasn't much left to remove. Kylie was shapely, with big tits and a nice bubble butt, and she was struggling to stay in her bikini. Marie was slim with little titties but also a nice arse. I would fuck them both if I could get my way and at the same time why not, given my adventures of late. I had been planning on visiting Sonia this weekend. Oh, the joys of group sex when you're used as a meat popsicle. I was looking forward to just fucking Sonia on her own. It was going to be magnificent as she was a real high-class woman. Anyway, I digress.

Marie and Kylie both jumped in the pool and swam about to cool off. I sat on the edge with my legs dangling in the water, watching them chatting away. Occasionally they whispered silently to each other, which seemed normal kind of, as after all I was a total stranger. We talked about university life, and they asked me about window cleaning. Marie asked if I'd ever been sprung naked in anyone else's home, and we all laughed. If only she knew. I plunged back in as it was just too hot a day and we continued to chat until Marie suggested we get out and have a smoke and a drink, so we all hopped out.

We sat around a small table in the shade of an umbrella and Marie lit up a joint. She inhaled gently and then lay back in her chair, handing the smoke to Kylie. Kylie puffed away and then it was my turn. I inhaled deeply, and it hit my head quickly. I also lay back and relaxed. I passed the joint to Marie and it went around until it was done, and we were well high. After a while Marie got up and went inside to get us all some drinks. I complimented Kylie as I figured it couldn't hurt to have a go and see where this ended up. She was pretty sexy, Kylie, and she loved the compliment. I told her that she looked great in the bikini and that she looked sexy. It was easier without them both there and high as I was, so I took my moment. She blushed and thanked me, smiling. I could tell she really liked my attention.

At that moment Marie opened the sliding door and asked if I could give her a hand. She couldn't get the bottle tops off. We all cracked up laughing. Bloody weed, it'll do that to you. I jumped up and headed inside, closing the door to keep out the heat. It was cool inside the house with the air conditioning running, and as I took off the bottle top, Marie asked me who I like most. I was a bit surprised, stunned. I mean, even this was a bit fast for me "Well, I don't know," I mumbled, not the greatest response but at least I was honest. Marie was quick to inform me that Kylie was really into me and wanted to make out, but Marie was wondering who I preferred as she was interested as well. The dope really was a leg opener.

Well, I'll be, the window cleaner strikes again, I thought to myself. Not wanting to upset Marie, I told her that I thought she was hot and I did. We began to kiss quite passionately. I felt her up nicely as she was only in a bikini and she gave me free access to do whatever I wanted. She enjoyed my arse as well, giving it a good squeeze. I could have fucked her in the kitchen but with Kylie outside, she stopped me and told me that Kylie would be upset. I quickly turned her around, bending her towards the bench, and went down for a chew on her arse. Pulling her bikini bottoms aside and spreading her cheeks, I dove in, licking her arse and pussy. I figured I'd give her a taste of what's to come. After a short taste I stopped and stood up. Breathing heavily, she looked at me wantonly. I grabbed the open bottles and suggested we head outside. She made me promise to not tell her that we'd just made out and that we could catch up later. This was crazy as I had just been warming Kylie up outside and I knew I could get her now, and truth be known I'd be happy fucking them both. I certainly wasn't going to commit to only one of them. I wasn't committing to anyone. I was going to go wherever my cock led me and at this stage I was feeling them both.

Marie and I headed outside and joined Kylie on the seats. Kylie was laying back, stretched right out with her legs crossed at her ankles and looking mighty. Her bikini was very tiny, and she was pretty much on show for all to see. She had hiked her bikini bottoms up high and was showing off the most spectacular VW bonnet up front. It was memorising and I perved on her heaps. It was easy to do as I had my bolles on and you couldn't tell where I was looking, at least that's what I thought. I didn't really care at this point, and I was certainly enjoying the view. Marie had brought out Bacardi and Coke as well as ice and glasses, and it went down well. I was not really a drinker of spirits usually, but being so hot and mixed with the Coke and the dope, it was going down easy. We were all enjoying the drink and relaxing and there was this crazy sexual tension I could feel. Marie kept looking at me and smiling and Kylie I could see and knew from Marie that she wanted me.

Marie asked me if I wanted some more smoke, meaning weed, and I said, "Sure, why not." This was turning into quite the afternoon. I knew once the girls had some more weed that I'd be fucking them in no time as in my experience it had always been a leg opener. We probably didn't even need it given the effects the Bacardi and earlier smoke was having, but why the hell not. Marie headed inside to organise the weed, so I suggested to Kylie we jump in the pool. As we cooled off, I made a move and pulled Kylie towards me. She was easy and loved me feeling her. We kissed a long pash and I gripped her arse, which was full and soft as she wrapped her legs around me, pressing against my stiffening cock. Marie returned, cooing, "Knock it off, you two. Get a room."

We separated and returned to the table while Marie lit up the joint. We were all laughing and out of it and the two of them were good to go, so I leant forward and started rubbing Kylie's feet. She moaned sweetly as I moved further up her legs, caressing them softly. I started to kiss her feet. At this point I felt Marie rubbing my back with her feet, which distracted me momentarily. She was asking me, "What about mine?" So I turned and started to kiss her feet. This was heating up fast. While kissing Marie's feet and moving up her legs, I felt Kylie grabbing at my cock, which was expanding rapidly in my footy shorts.

As I turned to help Kylie release my cock from my shorts so that she could appreciate it properly, Marie piped up, saying, "Let's settle this once and for all." I didn't know what she was talking about exactly but then thought they were getting jealous with each other over me. It didn't seem to matter, though, as now Kylie was sucking down hard on my cock and it felt great. She had pulled it out the side of my shorts. It always did come out very willingly as the shorts were stretchy, handy in a situation like this. Kylie was really giving it a good go when suddenly Marie was there and wanting some too. Wow, this was grouse. Had there ever been a luckier man? Kylie came up for air, looking all wanting and letting Marie have her turn. Marie sucked hard and fast, and I felt I would cum if I wasn't laying on my back. It always took me longer that way, but I wasn't comfortable, so I pushed her off and stood up so that I was standing right in front of both of them. What a glorious scene. I was standing looking down on these two beauties with my cock fully erect out the side of my shorts, pointing straight at them, both of them looking wanting and ready for whatever I wanted. To make things easier I pulled off my shorts.

My cock swung powerfully in their faces. Kylie took first turn and started where she left off. I squeezed on her tits and pulled off her top. At the same time Marie was looking up at me, licking my balls and leg. On noticing her I pulled my cock away from Kylie and gave it to Marie. She continued her sucking actions and took me as deeply as she could. Kylie waited patiently for her turn again. Watching this was incredible. I went back and forth with these two beauties devouring my cock, deep-throating too. It was spectacular. I swapped between them for a period until I eventually came with both of them getting a good amount of mess all over them as they eagerly sucked and licked it down. Jeez, the weed really did make girls easy, I remember thinking. At this point we all went for another swim as we were as hot as hell but now the girls needed their turn. I could feel I wasn't going to be let go until I fucked them both. So much for Marie not letting Kylie know we made out.

We went into a bedroom, and I gave them both oral until climax, at which point I was well and truly at full mast again. Ready to give them heaps, which is exactly what I did. I fucked them both hard, pumping like a wild man as the whole situation was wild. They played with each other and me, kissing and sucking as I hopped from one to the other and just kept slapping their arses and giving them a good fucking. Eventually I decided I'd had enough. I finished finally with Kylie doing it doggie style. We were all blissfully wrecked at this point, so we all returned for another swim and walked right into Clint. Uh-oh!

As we came out the back door naked, all of us, he was just standing right there stunned. Marie screamed, as did Kylie, and they both rushed for cover back inside. Me, however, all my clothes were outside, and I was acutely aware that I now had to get out of there. Clint screamed, "What are you doing?" He was pissed. I moved quickly, jumping across to the table and grabbing my shorts. I looked back towards Clint. I could see he was coming my way and he had death in his eyes. There was no time to fuck around so I bolted around the pool and put some distance between him and me. I was way too fast for him, which was just as well as he looked like he was going to kill me.

Once I had some space, I put on my shorts but that was all I had. My runners and shirt were over by the outside shower. Also my wallet and keys were there, so I had to get to them. I started to head to the gates, but Clint was blocking the way. He was shouting, "Wait till I get hold of you. You're never going to work on this side of the bridge ever again."

My only chance out was to run the other way and jump his side fence. It was risky as I would have to come close to him and grab my wallet and keys. Otherwise I wasn't going anywhere. There was no other way, so I went for it. As I got to the shower, Clint started heading my way as he realised what I was doing. I grabbed my wallet and the keys, not worrying about the rest, and headed quickly to the fence, gathering speed. I was not going to make it and we collided in a big collision that sent Clint flying backwards to the ground hard. I had dipped my shoulder into him as we met, like in a game of football. I could have kept running but seeing him fall so hard it made me stop to see if he was all right. I was in my footy prime and had really cleaned him right up. It was unintentional of course, but this was a matter of pure survival. He groaned on the ground as I asked if he was all right. "Fuck off," he said. "Get out of here."

I hastily went back and grabbed the rest of my things and headed out the gate to the van. Kylie, now dressed, ran out and met me, and after she gave me her phone number, I went on my way. The adrenaline was pumping as I drove down the road. What an afternoon I'd had. I was still high from the weed and booze and feeling great after getting my rocks off on a couple of nice new arses. Life was good. The radio was playing "The Heat Is On" from the *Beverly Hills Cop* soundtrack and it seemed fitting. Now that was a hoot as I sang and bopped away. As I returned the van to the office, I was a little paranoid from the smoke and the action and of course nervous about my possible dismissal. The boss, however, never said a thing. As I headed home, I only had two thoughts: notch another couple up to Mr Dick Pane, and Clint's words: "You'll never work on this side of the bridge again."

FROM THE JOURNAL

Today I fucked these two university girls Marie and Kylie after being busted in their backyard naked. I was working on this house and the owner said I could have a swim. Stupidly I swam naked, but it all worked out in the end with me scoring a double blowjob and then fucking them both. We got high on some weed and Bacardi as well and then Clint, Marie's dad, caught us all naked coming out to the pool. He wasn't happy and after trying to escape I ended up knocking him over before heading home, relieved for some sleep. He screamed at me that I would never work on that side of the bridge again. I couldn't care. Another happy day.

FROM THEN ON

I snuck over the bridge quite a few times after that and plugged away at both Kylie and Marie at different times. Never at Clint's house. The girls shared a flat, so we fucked there most of the time. I had to be careful when fucking Marie as Kylie really fell for me, but she was nothing more than a good casual root for me. I didn't want anything else. Marie liked me as well but realised I was a man whore and referred to me as such. She enjoyed the casual sex whenever we got together and knew it was nothing more than that. She was careful not to let Kylie know that we ever had sex other than the first time.

FINAL

So, there you have it, my first year as a window cleaner, and what a year it was. As Christmas approached, I continued my path of sexual mayhem and destruction—mostly the destruction of some lovely little delicious young or older woman's pussy. It had been a big year for me, especially sexually, as you no doubt now realise, and I was loving it. So as we broke from work for a few weeks over Christmas, the boss and the boys headed in different directions for a little holiday break. I thought to myself. *Well, what am I going to do?* I'll let you guess.

THE END

PS: If you think this year was crazy, then wait till you see what's to cum and I do mean cum.

9 780228 879992